Strange Metamorphosis

P. C. R. Monk

ISBN: 1-4800-0809-5
ISBN-13: 9781480008090

Bloomtree Press
pcrmonk@bloomtreepress.com

Dedication

For Anthony, Dylan and Lloyd

1

A Case of the Conscience

In a shabby brick cottage that sat on a plot where machines seemed to grow among the bushes, a teenage boy was tilting pensively on a wooden chair. The legs squeaked and bits of straw fell from the seating as he balanced deliciously over the center of gravity. It was his habit to loll back his head to one side to let his cat intermittently lick his dark thatch of hair. She was lounging half in the sun, half in the shade, on her tatty old cushion that lay among the various odd devices that intermingled with the other sideboard residents. In fact, virtually every surface of the cluttered dining room was occupied by "alternative ornaments": a sparkplug here, a bulb there, a piece of rubber tubing, an odd set of screws in a jar... Needless to say, the boy had a passion.

He sat with one foot outstretched and a big toe acting as a counter-stop beneath the lateral support of the dining table. This unlikely posture was quite possibly Marcel Dassaud's optimal thinking pose. Of course, some questions in life deserved such careful deliberation; their outcomes may have irreversible consequences.

***

Beautiful butterflies and gilded beetles adorned the walls in the plush furnished drawing room at Villeneuve. A bee bumbled insistently against the tall French windows as Philibert Deforge, the proprietor of the manor house, put down his newspaper and pulled out his pocket watch in exasperation.

'I'm sure he won't be long, dear. He's probably busy helping his mother,' said his wife peering over her spectacles while continuing her game of patience. 'She did say she might hang on a while and take the midday coach. Poor woman, she's quite prepared to let him go, but she always has been such a ditherer.'

Philibert Deforge sprang up from his high-backed armchair, rolled his paper into a club, and strode toward the bee with a watch-out-here-comes-the-bug-buster look on his face.

'Besides, he might be a boy wonder, but you know Marcel lives in a world of his own, Papa,' said Henriette, who broke off stumbling through her arpeggios at the grand piano in a corner of the room.

'Somewhere between planet auto and planet loco, that's where you'll find Marcel Dassaud,' said her cousin Julia, who sat beside her to turn the pages.

'I mean, have you ever known him to be on time?' continued Henriette. 'He never thinks about anyone else; it's just beyond him.'

'He does have mitigating circumstances,' said Madame Deforge.

'Like living in the country for one,' said Julia, who made it sound about as exciting as watching a parade of snails. Julia, a city girl through to the marrow, was unlikely to ever be reconciled with country life after being forced to leave Paris upon her father's sudden death and having sold her piano to help pay for the funeral. Not only did she lose her champion but also her dream of becoming a concert pianist.

'Hmm, he may have mitigating circumstances, but he shall have to learn that time stands still for no man and that it is never constant in its flight,' said Deforge in a Proustian outburst. Moving up slowly behind his daughter, he ordered: 'Now don't move. There's a bee on your bonnet, my girl.'

Henriette pursed her lips and held her breath.

'It probably wants to fly out,' said the self-possessed voice of Julia. But her uncle's paper truncheon went whizzing close to Henriette's large ear, which caused ruddy wisps of hair to float up wildly like spider threads. It wasn't long, though, before she had them under control and priggishly tucked them back into her plait.

'That's thirty love, to the bee,' said Julia, which earned her a glacial look of reproach from her cousin. 'Henriette, what? You're the one who keeps going on about the virtues of country life and the clever things bees do in it. You have to admit this one's got incredible talent; it's a very clever dodger. Forty love,' she said. DeForge gave a bullish grunt at the attempted witticism and with renewed grit swiped the air again. This time he swatted the creature full on against the marble table before knocking it to the floor and crushing its body under his heel. 'I'll rephrase that, it *was* a clever dodger, poor thing,' pursued Julia with a grimace creeping along her lip.

'Game, set, and match!' triumphed Deforge. 'Blasted things are everywhere!' He scooped the insect up and flicked it out of the window. Then to his wife he said, 'He hasn't mentioned anything yet then?'

'Nothing. But don't worry, dear. I suspect Marcel is not so absent-minded as to not see where his interests lie.'

'I wouldn't bank on it,' said Julia, returning her aunt's wry grin.

'That's true. I don't think he has any interest in anything except machines and bugs,' said Henriette glumly.

'Nonsense, the poor boy needs someone to look up to and a little stability, that's all. We'll soon have him as good a gentleman as your father,' said Madame Deforge, who then turned to her niece and said, 'Julia, make yourself useful and pass round the olives to your uncle.'

Philibert DeForge picked one from the outstretched dish then sat back down with his newspaper and spent the next few minutes trying to shake the words off the pages.

***

The frantic flutter of insect wings broke the boy's meditation. The cat stopped and stared up at the shaded corner between the pendulum clock and the wall where a butterfly was struggling to free itself from a spider's web. Marcel was particularly pleased with the spider's upkeep; its web had already proved an excellent mosquito trap.

He pulled quickly against the table with his toe to set the chair squarely back on its four legs. Then swiftly he went for his butterfly net. It was propped against the wall under the post office calendar that portrayed a pastoral scene and listed the months of the year 1911.

He was barely halfway back across the room when the butterfly, which turned out to be a moth, broke its tethers and fell back through the air before instantly regaining flight. It darted over the outstretched net straight for the mantelpiece. It took refuge behind a yellowing photograph of a man with an arm around a boy of nine, which had pride of place beside a funeral urn.

Slipping his fingers scissor-fashion behind the photo, Marcel brought out the moth, dangling from a clump of dusty spider web thread. He snatched up a matchbox from a collection conveniently piled in stacks on the sideboard and popped in his prize.

'What d'ya think of that then, Dad? I bet it's a humming bird sphinx,' said the boy, smiling triumphantly at the urn. 'Wait 'til ole Deforge sees this!' On turning his thoughts to Deforge and his offer of an apprenticeship at Villeneuve, Marcel said to himself,

'Hmm, and he'll be wanting an answer today, I bet. Can't keep putting him off.'

He put down the matchbox and pulled out an envelope from behind the urn. 'And what about this?' He sighed. It was a letter offering him a scholarship at a technical college in Paris.

Paris, the city of light. Paris, the city of the metropolitan railway. Paris, the city of a million workers. How could a country lad fit into it?

Putting on a deep voice, he said, 'Just tear it up and throw it in the bin, my boy...' Then the next instant, he added, 'What are you waiting for, Marcel? Where there's a will there's a way.' But alerted by footsteps in the corridor, his little act was cut short.

'Marcel, Marcel!'

Stuffing the envelope into his pocket, he turned to face a devout woman with tired eyes as she stepped into the room. 'You'd better get ready; they're expecting you at Villeneuve, remember. It's ever so nice of them to have you. Now give me a kiss. My coach'll be here in a minute. Are you sure you won't come to Lourdes with me?' said Madame Dassaud after a peck on the cheek from her only son, who was already half a head taller than she was. 'I'll be back on Sunday. Be good, Marcel, won't you,' she said, caressing his cheek, which showed signs that a young man was metamorphosing inside. 'And don't forget your hat; it's baking out. And don't forget your manners either, and don't swank—'

'Mom, I stopped teasing Henriette when I was nine.'

'I wasn't thinking of Henriette!' returned his mother with a sly eye. Thankfully, though, the familiar sound of the coach and horse clopping from out of the distance saved him from an awkward moment. 'Quick, here comes the coach for the station,' said Madame Dassaud. It stopped twice a day just opposite the little brick cottage.

Barely five minutes later, Marcel had put her case on the carriage and was waving her off.

'How did she guess about Julia?' he wondered as his feet carried him back through the cluttered dining room and into his mother's neat and clean-smelling bedroom. True, she was definitely attractive, both in the literal and figurative sense. There was something about her that made you want to be near her; maybe it was her cityness. At any rate, until she came along, he had frankly never thought that encounters of the feminine kind could be so captivating. He found himself resorting to all sorts of silly ploys just to brush by her: slipping last year's horse chestnuts down her back, adjusting her bicycle saddle for her, even playing croquet! And she had a strange power of making him promise anything. It was Julia who had gotten him to take the scholarship exam, it was Julia who had pestered him with revision during the holidays, and it was her name that kept bouncing through his brain.

He poured a sample of his mother's perfume into a small vial. The clock in the dining room chimed. Twelve thirty already. He quickly put on his blazer and boater, spat on his shoes, gave them a rub with a cuff, and raced off on his bicycle.

He swerved off the country lane between some impressive brick gateposts. He followed the leafy drive humming with bees. Then, between a plane tree and a magnificent old lime tree, he put down a foot for a moment to take in the handsome country house that stood before him with its colonnaded porch clad in wisteria.

'This is the life, from rags to riches, pal!' he murmured to himself as Chico the Pyrenean sheepdog came woofing out to greet him.

***

Two hours later, dampened piano music was spilling out onto the porch where a peacock was perched. It made as much a mess of the wide window ledge as Henriette Deforge was making of Chopin's Prelude No. 4. Laurence, the buxom maid with forearms like marrows, shooed it away and pulled the shutters ajar to preserve the relative freshness of the main hall. It had become her routine for the past twenty-five years to go round the house during the summer months and shield it from the afternoon heat. She presently came to the drawing room where after-lunch coffee had been served. It would have been senseless to sit outside with the sun at its zenith in what was expected to be the hottest day of the year so far.

Marcel was sitting at the mahogany leather-topped writing desk in the adjoining study where more beetles and butterflies adorned the walls in various advanced poses of yoga. He had opened his matchbox and was undertaking the delicate operation of removing spider thread from his live captive. Philibert Deforge, skittle-shaped, heavy-browed with large rubbery traits, stood peering over it holding the magnifying glass with one hand and intermittently stroking his ash-grey walrus moustache with the other.

'Fascinating, it's working; look, it's retracting its claws,' he said with gusto as Marcel dribbled another strand of saliva over the insect's hind legs. This dissolved the stickiness of the thread and enabled him to easily pull it away with his tweezers. The boy then held the insect up to the light, as if he were inspecting the workings of a pocket watch.

'Brilliant piece of engineering. Now keep still and be grateful; we're going to make you eternally beautiful,' he said to the moth as it kicked, writhed, and wriggled between the tweezer tips.

'Yes, fine specimen. Soon as you're done, we'll pop it straight into the barrel!' said Deforge. The "barrel" was a homemade gas chamber made by Marcel on Deforge's demand, where selected captives were put to sleep and preserved for pinning.

'I've recharged with that ethyl acetate, by the way. It's true it doesn't discolor the specimen like cyanide. You have to watch it though, takes a bit longer to kill,' said the boy.

'I noticed. The other day, I netted one of them giant hornets they've been going on about. Born killers. Thought the bloody thing was dead, and it turned around and bit me,' said Deforge, looping a sardonic grin at the pinned specimen on the bureau, which made his heavy jowls wobble.

Through the open doors in the drawing room, Julia sat beside Henriette on the piano seat, indolently following the score. Another false note in the middle of the stretto and Julia, who ground her teeth again, strode over to the study threshold and stood watching the operation with one finger placed in the ear nearest the piano.

'Having fun?' said Marcel without looking up.

'Oh, time just flies by, must be the country living. I mean you wouldn't believe I've been sitting there turning the pages since before lunch, would you?' said Julia, who made it sound excruciatingly exciting. 'Oh, poor little butterfly, why are you torturing it?'

'It's a moth. I'm cleaning it for the collection; better than ending up like any old bug in any old field.'

'How cruel!'

'Pshhht,' snapped her uncle.

But another dodgy chord made her wince and give out a little painful groan in spite of herself. This prompted Marcel to look up and release his hold of the tweezers. The moth, instantly rediscovering the use of its legs and realizing it wouldn't get another chance, leapt into the air and took flight.

'Close all the windows, quick!' fired Deforge as the boy bustled around the obstructive person of Julia toward the French windows that led from the drawing room out into the garden. The moth was no fluttery butterfly; it had plans, and it zoomed as straight as a bolt between the windows just as Marcel reached for the handle.

'Hard luck!' said Julia with a jubilant clap of the hands.

'Blast it! That was a humming bird sphinx. I've only got two of those!' said Deforge, turning to the specimens in their glass tombs above the drawing room mantle.

'Sorry, Monsieur Deforge, I lost my concentration,' said Marcel, taking it out on a fly buzzing round his ears.

'Yes, it is a disappointment, but it isn't your fault, though. I should have closed the doors to avoid intruders,' said Deforge, focusing his thunderous gaze toward Julia. 'But, well, what's done cannot be undone, can it?'

Julia was about to counter the offensive when Henriette, oblivious to all the commotion she had indirectly caused, at last came to the end of her romantic prelude.

'Bravo!' called Madame Deforge, who put down her illustrated journal of Parisian high-society and clapped her hands.

Julia joined in the applause. Then, arching her joined fingers, she said, 'Getting there, cousin. Move over. My turn now.'

'No, I think that's enough clumping on that blasted piano for now,' said Deforge in a foul mood. And with something visibly on his mind, he stepped back into his den.

'She's been practicing for her lesson,' corrected Madame Deforge, peering over her spectacles after him.

'You wouldn't think it, though, would you,' said Julia with a sour grin. She regretted the slip of the tongue the moment it was out, but she had been patiently waiting all this time to play herself. For Julia, playing the piano was something spiritual, something like food for the soul. Something that could make her irritable beyond reason if she went without too long. And if Henriette had happily conceded to her needs when she first moved near Villeneuve with her mother some months back, strangely now she more and more offered resistance. In a fleeting instant, it occurred to her that Henriette had become jealous, that she deliberately used the lessons as an excuse for keeping her away from the piano. But that piano meant self-preservation. If she could no longer play it, she would go insane.

She wished she had bit her tongue instead of becoming prey to her rotten temper again. So trying to make up for the slip, she added, 'I mean, she ought to be given more time between lessons. Wilfried only came a few days ago.'

'That's because I'm preparing a piece for my birthday party. I already told you,' said Henriette with a stabbing gawk. 'And I bet you're just saying that so you can hog my piano.'

'Hog your piano? You never used to be that passionate about it,' said Julia, trying to laugh it off.

'How could I with you on it all day long showing off your arpeggios and being superior, even to Wilfried.'

'It's not exactly difficult to be superior to Wilfried,' remarked Marcel, holding out his hands on the sides of his head like an extension to his ears and forcing his incisors over his lower lip. It was Marcel's impersonation of Wilfried Delpech, Henriette's piano teacher, and it was true. If we all had our alter ego in the animal kingdom, Wilfried's would most certainly be a docile donkey, always ready to serve.

'I wasn't superior to Wilfried at all; in fact, I happen to like his style,' said Julia. 'He has a natural way of playing with his big bony hands. He plays like…well, like—'

'Like a country bumpkin. Go on, say it, miss city girl.'

'No, actually I was going to say like a craftsman, because he plays with such method. His hands cover the keyboard in such a way it seems he hardly has to move them, if you really want to know. Or haven't *you* noticed?'

'Anyway, I'd rather you didn't insist on showing off to him from now on. It takes up all my lesson time.'

'That's all right by me. I don't mind playing before he comes,' said Julia, not letting her desperation show through her naturally confident bearing.

'Girls, girls,' said an elderly lady rousing from her after-coffee nap, 'you remind me of your mothers.' It was Henriette and Julia's grandmother. 'I say, does that mean Father Brulin's coming, too?' she said in a sing-song voice.

'Yes, mother,' said Madame Deforge, 'if Wilfried is coming, then Father Brulin must be coming for tea. You ought to know that by now.'

In actual fact, it was the other way round. Wilfried, who played the church organ, escorted Father Brulin whenever he came to tea. In fact, it was the old priest who first suggested Wilfried as piano teacher, no doubt to earn the lad a bit of extra cash and perhaps to bring Henriette out of her shell. Father Brulin was a fine judge of character.

'Oh, I am pleased. He has such nice manners. But that young man with the flat feet does glare at you, dear.'

'Me?' said Henriette with flushing cheeks.

'Don't tell me you haven't noticed.'

'That's silly, Grandma. He's my piano teacher. Besides, he's hardly one of us, is he?'

'Henriette, what a snob you are,' said Julia.

'No, I'm not. I've invited him to my birthday party,' said Henriette, as proof that she wasn't.

'And speaking of birthday parties,' said Madame Deforge, 'Marcel, it would be so lovely if you announced your apprenticeship to everyone on Saturday, too.'

Marcel looked round donkey-like and utterly at a loss for words. Of course he was half expecting someone to pop the question, but he still wasn't ready for it. In the seconds it took for him to find his tongue, he weighed the pros and cons of starting at Villeneuve or taking up the scholarship in the city. But there he was—maybe it was fate, maybe it was providence—at any rate, he was glad to make the decision at last.

'Um, well, y-yes, I s'pose I could,' he spluttered.

His acceptance was instantly met with a cheerier Deforge, who strode back out of his study and said, 'Excellent, my boy, it would make it official.'

Julia, on the other hand, turned wordlessly to Marcel with the sheen of reproach, grumbled something about visiting the first sunflowers on Mon Plaisir field, and stomped out of the room.

'Pick three for the vase, Julia,' called Madame Deforge after her. It was for tradition's sake, three of the season's first sunflowers were always placed on the dining room table.

'So here's to another Dassaud on the payroll!' continued Deforge, raising his coffee cup and touching Marcel on the shoulder. 'I was beginning to wonder if you were going to accept, ha—'

'Nonsense, dear. Marcel just needed a little prompting, didn't you, Marcel?' said Madame Deforge in a ring of triumph.

'Er, y-es,' conceded the boy, whose thoughts had flown out of the room with Julia.

Monsieur Deforge had picked up the pinned giant hornet and activated its jaws. 'Look, this is the little beast that bit me, the tiger of insects,' he said. 'Terrifying beggars they are; look at those mandibles. Just a handful of them can decimate an entire bee colony. Dead as a dodo now, though, hah.'

After further inspection of the unique trophy, visibly with other thoughts on his mind, Marcel said, 'If you don't mind, I thought I'd go net some butterflies before Malzac mows the park.'

'Good, my boy, you'll find the killing jar with the net out front.'

***

A few moments later, Marcel was standing on the colonnaded porch beneath the draping wisteria where he found Deforge's jar and insect net in a corner. Julia was sitting on the wicker chair.

'Hey, penny for your thoughts,' he ventured, waving his boater hat in front of her eyes.

'I wouldn't ask if I were you, Marcel Dassaud, and you know what I mean!' she said getting brusquely to her feet.

'What?' Marcel gave a guilty glance down at his hand holding the killing jar. 'I told you, they don't feel a thing, and neither would you if you wore your skeleton inside out—'

'You know what I mean; why didn't you tell them about the bursary?'

'Oh, that,' Marcel replied, trying to pass it off, which made Julia's eyes blaze even more.

'Yes, that! Huh, I bet you didn't really even pass it, cause no one in their right mind would turn down a scholarship, which is probably why of late you've stopped working on machines and started killing insects instead.'

'Collecting, actually.'

'Killing, collecting, same thing.'

'All right, look for yourself if you don't believe me.' Marcel pulled out the letter of acceptance. Julia snatched it from him and ran her eyes over its contents. The relief of having earlier stuffed the letter in his pocket put a smile in his voice when he said, 'Told you. Look, I'm sorry, Julia. I know I said some wild things about wanting to make it big and all that, but, well, maybe I just needed to prove I was capable of it, and, well, with that I don't need to now, do I? Besides, my place is here. This is where my dad worked. Come on, it isn't that bad. In fact it's a brilliant opportunity. Don't look at me like that, Julia.' But Julia gave no answer. 'By the way— look—I've got a present for you. It's your favorite,' he pursued brightly, bringing the vial of perfume from his inner jacket pocket. But she left his hand outstretched.

'Marcel, you just haven't got it, have you?' she said at last. 'Passing that exam only means there's potential in you; it's just the first step on the ladder. Now you've got to climb up it!'

That took the smile off his lips and brought a sudden flush to his cheeks as he said, 'What about Monsieur Deforge? I can't let him down now, can I?'

'You can't always be what other people want you to be. For one, most of them just want you to fit into their conception of the world; most of them just don't care whether you fulfill your destiny or not. There are a great many people like that, Marcel. You've got to resist being taken over by their personal ambitions for you. Someone once told me that if you give up your passion for the sake of living up to peoples' expectations, then you can wave your true destiny good-bye. But of course you could always stick around here and just become like any old bug in any old field, couldn't you!'

'You're just saying that. You don't like it here anyway. And I'm no Parisian. This is my home.'

'Excuses. In my opinion, you're just afraid of failing! And to think I actually believed what you said about your dream of building cars and making something of yourself. Well I wish I'd never got you to take that exam in the first place, Marcel Dassaud. I thought you had some talent, but I didn't realize you had absolutely no ambition, or is it another kind of ambition you're planning? Which would explain your trying to worm your way into Villeneuve. Here's your letter and as for your perfume, why don't you give it to Henriette!'

'Julia, Julia,' called Marcel, trying to keep his voice down.

'Just…buzz off!' she growled under her breath and marched off round the corner of the house in the direction of the sunflowers on Mon Plaisir field.

Girls, why do they get so emotional? he thought in an effort to distance her judgment. But he still felt his belly churning over, like he had chickened out of a dare. He was wondering whether he ought to go after her when a movement from behind the hall windows caught his eye and relieved him for the moment of tackling his awkward feelings. It was Madame Deforge who moved forward into the window frame. Quickly slipping the vial and the letter back into his pockets, he returned a fake smile and ostentatiously reached for the butterfly net, put the string attached to the killing jar around his neck, and went on his own way.

2
The Great Oak Tree

He let his stride carry him past the magnificent cedar tree where the peacock was proudly preening its feathers on a low bough. Then he walked across the alley of horse chestnut trees and over the sun-splayed meadow toward the thick shade of the grand old oak, a veritable monument of nature.

Many a time he had climbed it to where the trunk ramified into seven solid branches. There he would sit seven meters up, inventing things in the mossy pit while his father, the late steward of the manor grounds, went over the accounts with Monsieur Deforge. A smile crept along the boy's lips as he recalled his dad whispering in his ear that it was a magic tree, a wise tree in which you could confide a momentous secret or share the burden of a cogged-up mind.

The great tree, which measured a staggering twelve meters in girth, was over a thousand years old, the earliest mention of its existence being recorded in the local cadaster of 1096 as the wise man's oak past which the road runs to Jerusalem. The wise man in question was the just and revered Guy Darasus, an herbalist versed in the secrets of plants and a wise counselor by nature. According to the legend, at the close of his life, local folk asked him where they could turn for support and advice when he was gone. So the old sage arranged for his body to be buried beneath the already twice centenarian oak in the promise that his wisdom and counsel be passed into its grain. In this way, on his deathbed he was able to vow that those brave enough to confront their conscience beneath the tree's boughs may find guidance and peace within.

Some strange fairy tale thought the pragmatic lad as he strolled up to the foot of the tree. Though he had to admit it was certainly true that he had found no place better for comfort and inspiration.

Marcel placed his hat and parked his posterior on the plinth of a Virgin Mary statue. He propped his net beside him and steered his thoughts back to his single most favorite subject: his Vroomster, a fabulous 4-cylinder 1500 cc automobile, which he believed would replace the horse and cart and take even the humblest of humanity rolling effortlessly into the twentieth century.

It wasn't long, though, before something else came nudging its way between thoughts. That two-faced dilemma he had been trying to ignore over the last weeks was back and now wearing Madame Deforge's smirk of triumph on one side and Julia's blazing glare on the other.

All right, being awarded a scholarship was quite an achievement for someone not yet fifteen, but what of it? It would mean going to the city, where he knew no one, and competing with the street-wise city kids. It would make things easier if at least he could know if he had it in him to rise to the challenge. And what about Deforge, who expected him to start on the estate? True, it was a rare opportunity for one of his humble background, not to mention one that would enable him to stay at home. And he would have happily walked into it if Julia had not come along and talked him into taking the scholarship exam. The last post to send off his acceptance fell at noon Saturday next, ironically the same day as Henriette's birthday party.

'Well, should I stay or should I go?' he said to himself, gazing up toward the pit of the tree.

Of course there was no answer amid the summer song of cicadas; only the rustle of green leaves whispered in the boy's ear as he watched the sun filter through them. But then the tree began to creak. This was followed by a gut-churning crack of timber as the whisperings grew into a deafening crescendo. Marcel suddenly felt his blood course through his veins. An ominous shiver bolted down his spine and rooted him to the spot. He then became aware that the low boughs were growing higher and higher, that the tree's trunk was growing fatter and fatter, that it was all shooting up before his very eyes. He shook his head, screwed his fists into his eye sockets, and again looked up in wonder at the thick boughs that now seemed a thousand meters above his head, until, looking round toward the house, the boy at last realized that in fact the tree had not grown at all. Judging by the canopy of giant grasses that lay before him, it dawned on him that he had shrunk!

3

A Message in an Oak Apple

He found himself on top of the plinth, lodged in a fold of the statue's plaster of Paris robe, near its right foot.

'Crikey, what's happened to me?' he deplored in horror as he got to his feet. 'I can't be more than two centimeters tall! What will Deforge say?' he fretted, measuring himself against his boater. But his panic attack gave way to sheer terror the moment he looked over the ledge at the mosaic slab on the ground below. It was like he was standing on the plinth of the Statue of Liberty. Then, caught between consternation and anger, he coiled back into the fold and howled out above him: *'Why is this happening to me? What have I done?'*

There was no answer. Nothing else happened. Pulling himself together, he stood up again with a resolute stamp. 'No, this is impossible, this-is-im-poss-ible,' he said, hammering out the syllables to make them ring true. 'This cannot be happening. I must be dreaming; I am dreaming, come on,' he said, braving a step out from the fold. 'I know…if I stand on one foot and count to five, I'll wake up.' But he had not got past four when someone took the next word out of his mouth.

'Five thousand and seventy six, five thousand and seventy five.' Marcel nearly stumbled clean over the plinth as he looked over at the nearby hawthorn bush. A brownish caterpillar resembling a twig was counting its strides as it looped its way down the stem. The boy steadied his stance and stood gawking at the insect. Even though there were at least two meters between them, he was fascinated to find he could make out every detail as clearly as looking through a magnifying glass: the outgrowth on the creature's back, the pores on the side of its abdomen where it took in air. He was wondering if he had ever seen anything quite so hideous when the caterpillar suddenly stopped its descent, looked up from a lush leaf, and said, 'Watchoo stawing at?' It had a language impediment that, transcribed from the vernacular, was comparable to it putting a *w* in place of a consonant *r*.

'Wow, this is just crazy. So I did hear you talk!'

'Talk? Course I can talk. It's a wonder how you can, though, without any antennas!'

'Euh? But you're a brimstone caterpillar.'

'I beg your pardon, young sir, I'm an inchworm, born of a family of geometers,' said the insect before nibbling into another juicy leaf.

'Of course, sorry, my mistake. Yes, a brimstone inchworm—'

'But you can call me plain Bwimstone, or Bwim for short. What do they call you then?'

'Er, well, I'm a human. But you can call me Marcel if you like.'

'I've always wanted to meet a marcel,' said the inchworm. 'I must admit, though, I always thought they were taller.'

'I am taller, normally, but I've shrunk.'

'Huh, I bet that's what they all say.'

'No, but it is true; I've been shrunk. Listen, Brimstone, I can hardly stay like this. I've really got to grow back and quick. See, I've got to go to a girlfriend's birthday party in a few days. What would she think?'

'I do know how you feel, Marcel. I mean, the things you have to go thwough to attwact so much as a glance fwom the faiwer sex. Well, you'll just have to do as I do, keep on munching and moving 'til you've built yourself up enough to find a nice comfy place to change into your courting suit.'

'But I'm not going anywhere; I'm stuck on this blasted plinth. Unless I slide down this here,' said Marcel, whose eye had caught a thin, twisted cord glistening in the sun. It ran from above his head down to a box tree stem near the ground. With renewed spirit he began to climb up the big toe of the statue of the Virgin Mary to get a good grasp of the line.

''Ang on a sec,' said Brimstone. 'Do marcels eat inchworms?'

'No, they don't.'

'That's good.'

'Why?'

'Just inquiwing. And by the way, I wouldn't go for that thwead if I was you, belongs to that gweat fat spider up there, see?'

Lifting his eyes, Marcel suddenly became aware of a whole network of threads further above his head. There was an extra long one leading up to a hollow in the statue's plaster drape where it took its source. It sent a shudder of dread from the boy's hair follicles down to his curling toes. At the edge of the hollow, he saw four pairs of black beady eyes gleaming out and the long hairy leg of the tenant placed upon the thread, waiting for a bite, as you might say.

'And word's out the wench has nothing left in her larder, if you see what I mean,' said the inchworm with a shudder. He was referring to the vampirized corpses still snugly clad in silk jackets near the middle of the web. 'Sucks the body fluids out of 'em, she does.'

Marcel gave a forlorn shrug of the shoulders and let himself drop back to where he had started.

'Can't marcels cwawl down walls then?' asked the inchworm.

'No, marcels can't crawl down walls, Brimstone,' returned Marcel curtly.

'Well, can ya fly?'

'Nope, I can't fly. I haven't got wings, or haven't you noticed?'

'Oh. I don't know what to suggest then. Maybe you ought to twy using your bwain. I've been told marcels have got good bwains on 'em. Anyway, sowwy I can't help. I've a pwessing engagement myself. Now, where was I? Five thousand and seventy four, five thousand and seventy thwee…'

The inchworm went on looping his way down the hawthorn bush, sampling the luscious leaves as he went. Upon the plinth, Marcel let himself drop on a lump of moss, and he sat there, elbows on knees, head wedged in hands. 'All right for dumb caterpillars,' he said to himself, thinking of the inchworm's ability to crawl down stalks headfirst.

He backtracked through his mind. One minute he was wondering about his future and the next he was talking face-to-face with a bug. His thoughts inevitably turned to the legend of the tree. *Those brave enough to confront their conscience beneath its boughs may find guidance and peace within.* Then he burst out, 'All right, tree, supposing this is happening, what am I supposed to do now?'

But before he had time to dwell on his predicament, a knocking in the branches above made him lift his chin. His eye was immediately seized by a ball plummeting through the leaves. And more precisely, to the very spot he was sitting! For the life of him, he made a dash and a dive to a fold in the plaster robe hem just before the sphere exploded his mossy cushion. It then bounded off the plinth onto the mosaic slab on the ground far below.

Marcel pulled himself out of the fold, glad to still be in one piece. 'Phew, close shave, that!' he uttered, brushing down his jacket. He gave the big toe of the statue a comradely pat and went quickly to peer over the ledge of the plinth. Down at the mosaic base, he saw an oak apple that had come to rest, not for long though.

Marcel knew from experiments with his penknife that the oak apple, or gall, harbored a grub, which evolved into a tiny winged creature called a Cynips, otherwise known as a gallfly. He soon realized that he was about to witness one emerging from its lodge. No sooner had he found a safer and more comfortable position lying face down with his torso propped up on his elbows than the tawny ball began to tilt and topple slightly. Then there came a light scratching, and the first specs of gall dust were pushed out of a little hole from inside. A moment later, there came the black head, long antennae, the thorax, and the shapely abdomen easing out of its capsule into the great wide world. The insect rubbed her pretty head, buzzed her lattice-leaf wings, and looked up right at the ledge where Marcel lay looking on in wonder.

'I've a message for you,' she called in a soft trill.

'A message, oh, a message for me?' returned Marcel, sitting up straight in a glimmer of hope.

'Yes, the tree sent me,' said the gallfly. Proudly spreading her wings, she flew up into the sunshine toward him. 'To tell you how to gro—'

Marcel immediately realized that she had not noticed the spider's thread suspended in her path. He suddenly became aware that it must be virtually invisible from her point of view on the backdrop of the sky.

'No, get back! Don't come any closer!' he called out, jumping to his feet, horrified that what could be his only hope of escape was about to set foot in a deadly trap.

'Don't worry. I'm only a gallfly, and I mean you no harm,' she called, trying to sound reassuring though hovering closer still to the sticky thread.

'Stay back! There's a web!'

'A what?' But it was too late; she had put a foot in it, or rather, a tarsus, which is the specialist's term for an insect's foot.

'Don't move!' called Marcel anticipating her fright, 'or you'll alert the spider!'

'Oh, no, I'm stuck, I'm stuck!' lamented the insect, trying to pull her tarsus from the sticky thread, but then she got another one stuck.

'Oh, no.'

'Keep still, stop flapping, and play dead!'

'But—'

'Or the spider's going to eat you!' With that, the gallfly suddenly froze and let herself hang upside down from her ensnared claws. 'That's better. Now stay nice and calm, Gallfly, and tell me what the tree told you.'

'Please, help!' she trilled, ignoring his request.

'I can't,' he returned. 'I'm stuck here myself, but if you tell me how I can grow, then I'll be able to help you.'

'I can't. I can't think,' said the petrified creature, who began to whimper.

Marcel gave a dubious glance over the ledge of the plinth to where the gallfly was dangling in midair, then up at the hollow where the diadem spider had her hairy foreleg placed on her telegraph wire. 'I can't do this,' he said to himself, even though he knew there was no other way if he wanted to get back to normalness. Swallowing another anxious gulp, he said, 'Right. Just keep quiet and don't move. I'm coming to get you, Gallfly.'

He climbed onto the statue's big toe, spat on his hands, and reached up for the silky strand that ran down parallel to the thread from which the gallfly was hanging.

'Just keep still now. You hear me, Gallfly? She may be half blind, but she'll be over in a flash if she detects you!'

He carefully slid his way along the twisted thread, spitting on his hands every few lengths to keep them from sticking, while trying his best not to make the line quiver. His strength seemed astonishingly boundless. At least he hardly felt his weight in his arms at all and found he could easily hang one-handed onto the thread and still lift up his body.

With new confidence and precision in his movements, he was soon level with the strand that held the gallfly prisoner.

'Well, how do you do?' he said, quite sure of himself now. He even let his eyes fleetingly admire the anatomy of the tiny insect that, incidentally, was as long as his arm!

'Do what?' she replied.

'Er? Oh, nothing, that's just a nice way of saying hello.'

'Well, if you don't mind, it would be nicer if you stopped looking under my wings!' trilled the gallfly, not forgetting her amour-propre despite the uncomfortable position.

'Oh, sorry. Right,' said Marcel, shaking himself back to the urgency of the situation. 'I'm going to cut the thread from around your feet,' he explained. 'So get ready to fly off!'

Marcel reached for his penknife in his pocket and proceeded to cut the claws free while dangling by one hand a breath-stopping twenty-five times his own height above the ground. As soon as one foot was free, the gallfly activated her tarsal segments to make sure all was in proper working order.

'Yuk, it's still sticky!' complained the insect.

'When you get free, spit on it, and you'll take the stickiness away,' said Marcel while keeping his eyes focused on carefully cutting away the claws of the other foot.

Meantime, little less than three meters further up, in her den, the spider placed her forefoot more firmly on the wire, as if to analyze the slight twitching movements issuing from the web. Up until now, these tremors could have been interpreted as belonging to a fallen leaf caught and trembling with the movement of the air, but...

'Easy does it, nice and slow,' said Marcel, as much to reassure himself as the gallfly. 'Now brace yourself; one more strand and you're free. There.'

The release of the gallfly sent a treacherous quiver up the line. Its impact was immediate. The spider came darting out of her den, down to where Marcel was desperately swinging back to the sanctuary of Saint Mary's big plaster toe.

'Jump!' shrilled the gallfly, now flying at Marcel's side.

'I can't,' cried Marcel with one eye on the approaching vile monster. It became clear he would have to face the abominable creature. So again, he reached in his pocket for his penknife, this time for his survival.

'Jump,' insisted the gallfly, 'it's your only chance!' Marcel gave a last glance from the terrifying creature to the ground a long way down. Just as he did so, the spider made a dastardly pounce. The instant its bristly tarsus touched the back of the boy's hand, his instinct made him let go of the thread. The next moment he was freefalling through the air with the gallfly at his side grinning her relief.

'Wow, that was a real whizzer!' she trilled, and the boy landed with a splodge.

At length Marcel looked up from the soft dome that had cushioned his fall and inwardly thanked Mother Nature for puffballs.

'It's revolting. Fancy being wrapped up in this stuff,' said the gallfly, landing next to him, only too glad to sink her claws into the moist dome to rid them of their stickiness.

'Well let that be a lesson to you, Gallfly. Never say die, eh?' said Marcel, pocketing his knife. 'Remember. Where there's a will, there's a way. Got it?'

'A will? What's a will?' questioned the gallfly, rubbing her feet together to rid them of the last strands of thread.

'A will? Oh, well, it's something you need if you want to achieve something.'

'What's it look like then?'

'It doesn't actually look like anything. In fact, you can't actually see it.'

'Is it so small then?'

'That's just the magic of it; even though it doesn't weigh a thing, and it doesn't cost a kopeck, it can lead you to great achievements. It can make a small man great, a poor man rich, or turn an ordinary man into a hero. See, will is the power of the mind. It lets us act beyond our condition.'

'Wow! I wish I had a will.'

'But you have, Gallfly. See, you willed me into jumping, even though I can't fly.'

'You can't fly?' said the gallfly with a pause in her diligent washing.

'Of course not, but you willed me to let myself drop onto the puffball, didn't you?'

'Did I? I didn't notice it until you landed on it, actually. Though I must admit, I did think you came down with a bit of a splodge.'

'Eugh?' uttered Marcel, pretty rocked that his life could have ended right there.

'Anyway, lucky you're better at willing than flying, or else I could never have delivered my message,' said the gallfly, who had finished preening herself.

'Yes, the message,' said the boy eagerly.

'The tree says that if you want to grow back, then you must eat some freshly made royal jelly before the sun rises three times.'

'Royal jelly? The stuff bees make?'

'Yep, the stuff that turns an ordinary grub into a queen bee.'

'Can't you get some for me, Gallfly? I've an important engagement in three days and I haven't prepared anything for it,' said Marcel, hoping that saving the insect's life entitled him to a favor.

But the gallfly, who was not one for beating about the bush, said, 'Sorry, I can't. Royal jelly is guarded by bees, and bees don't share it with gallflies. It's physical—'

'I have to get it myself, in other words,' said Marcel, pouting out his mouth.

'Yep, after all, it's your quest. I've enough with my own to think about. Don't worry, though, the more changes you make, the better you'll fit into bug life.'

'Changes?'

'Yes, the more you find out about yourself, the more you'll change. The good news is that each change will give you extra strength to help you find the royal jelly.'

'Hmm, I don't like the sound of that,' said the boy uneasily.

'You have to change, Marcel. Everyone does it; it's all a part of growing up, you know. Unless you'd rather stick around here and just become any old bug in any old field—your choice.'

'This is getting crazier by the minute. Look, Gall-fly, can you at least tell me which way I should look?'

'Sorry, I'm new to the neighborhood myself.'

'That's true, I s'pose,' conceded Marcel, placing chin on hand, hand on knee, upon the mushroom dome.

'Anyway, I must be flying. I've thousands of eggs to lay before the end of the busy season, you know. But remember what you said, *Where there's a will there's a way*, eh?' And off flew the gallfly to lay the season's generation of Cynips.

***

Vacantly sitting on the puffball dome, Marcel soon found himself reflecting on the immeasurable task the little insect now embarked upon. He suddenly felt even smaller than he was and quite ashamed of his momentary lack of grit. But then something mustered inside his chest at the recollection of his rescue feat. Not only had he the satisfaction of saving the tiny life, he had also learned something crucial about himself: he was no coward. He began to feel a fighting spirit he never knew he had as he recalled the words the brave little gallfly had echoed—an expression remembered from his father, and one he had come to use all too indifferently of late—before she flew off to lay how many eggs was it?

'Five thousand and twenty the-wee, five thousand and twenty two... *I* could have told ya that!' said a voice he knew.

4
Marcel Gets a Guide

'Anyone knows woyal jelly'll make a pwince out of a pauper. It's just getting at it that's the pwoblem!'

'Brimstone!' exclaimed Marcel, glad to see a familiar face, or at least a recently familiar one. 'But where can I find some royal jelly?'

'Hmmm, I might know. There again, I might not, depends, see,' returned the inchworm, bunching up his back and rumbling his short legs on the sunbaked ground in a reckoning sort of way.

'That's taking unfair advantage!' protested Marcel.

'Oh, no, Marcel,' returned the inchworm, now opening out his front legs in a reasoning sort of way. 'Don't get me wong. All I ask is to join you on your twavels. I'll be your personal guide. You're gonna be needing one, especially with so many pwedators in the field. It's a bug-eat-bug world here, you know. Plus, I do all my own feeding, and you can pay me only on aw-wival. How's that?'

Sitting up on the soft and spongy puffball dome, Marcel plunged his hands into his trouser pockets and turned out one penknife, one pocket watch, and two empty linings. 'Sorry, Brim, all I can offer you is my penknife, the time of day, and my name,' he said.

'For the moment, Marcel, for the moment,' said the inchworm with a knowing eye. 'But in the not too distant future, with your bwains and expert guidance from yours twuly, you'll be having your gwubbers on some wight woyal jelly. All I ask in weturn for my loyal services is a tarsus-ful of the noble nectar,' said the inchworm with a passionate glow in his eyes.

'And what would you want royal jelly for?' asked Marcel, amused at the creature's fervor.

'Let's just say to wectify that little ingwedient that Mother Nature overlooked on the cweation of my species.'

'And what's that?'

'Color, Marcel. Color to make the wings dazzle and catch the eye, if you see what I mean, something more pwincely. Just look at your good self for example—blue, yellow, a dash of white here, a splash of wed there— what a fine appawel She's given you. Me, I'll be lucky if I end up with a bwown tinge!'

Marcel couldn't resist a chortle as he let himself slide down the puffball dome, which delivered him smartly opposite the caterpillar. 'All right, Brimstone, you've got yourself a deal. You lead me to the royal jelly, and you shall have your share!'

'Bwilliant! You won't regwet it; I pwomise. Let's shake on it!' cheered the insect, who then offered three right-hand stubby appendages.

'Oh, yeah, right,' said the boy and shook each one of them in turn, thinking that this was decidedly turning out to be a strange kind of day but one that, he was now pleased to see, would soon end in a more normal sort of way. 'Now please take me to some fresh royal jelly,' he continued, already warming to the prospect of a larger perspective.

'The first thing to do,' began the inchworm in all the earnestness of a worthy guide, 'the first thing to do is to ask a bee.'

There followed a short pause for the penny to drop. At last Marcel spoke. 'You mean you don't actually know where the royal jelly is? I thought we agreed you'd guide me to some—'

'Oh, no, no, Marcel. We agweed I'd be your guide, and that's pwecisely what I shall do, guide you to a bee who'll tell us where to find some woyal jelly. And it just so happens that I know how to speak to bees. Not everybody can, you know. Can you speak to bees, mmm?'

'No, I don't suppose I can, not that I've ever tried, though.'

Marcel, who was beginning to get that sinking feeling that things would not turn out quite so easily after all, was at least comforted in the knowledge that one step in the right direction was better than any number in the wrong. So, recalling his pressing engagement, with an idea in mind, he urged his newfound guide to take him to a bee.

'Behind the tree there's a field, and in the field I know there's some sunflowers just opening. There must be bees there.'

The inchworm directed his antennae in the direction the boy was pointing. 'You sure? I can't smell anything,' he said. 'How far?'

Marcel did a quick sum in his head. If he stood about two centimeters tall, then one step would be equal to about one centimeter. And the field was about three hundred meters away. 'About thirty thousand steps in that direction,' he said with a slump in his voice in the realization that three hundred meters in his present condition was equal to thirty kilometers.

'I thought you said you were in a huwwy. Unless you've got wings, Marcel, it'll take you a lifetime to get there. No, our best bet's hopping along to the flowers on the meadow. You're bound to bump into one there. Mind, you'll have to watch yourself though,' warned the inchworm, and a lethal dart pricked Marcel's mind.

'You mean because of their sting?'

'Good 'eavens, no, because they don't always fly vewy stwaight, especially when their shopping baskets are full up. If you hear a buzzing overhead, wemember to duck!'

So off Marcel wended with the inchworm over the ground between dead leaves that sat as large as boats, twigs that could just as well have been tree trunks, and last season's acorns that lay littered here and there like great boulders. Until at last, they came to the limit of the shade of the great oak tree.

The sunshine blazed down on the tall grass, which gradually became as thick as a bamboo jungle, making it increasingly difficult to weave through. Still, Marcel forged ahead under the beating sun, while the inchworm counted his strides in his usual fashion, stopping every score or so for a nibble at a fresh green shoot.

'Come on, Brim,' called Marcel, turning round again to his guide gourmand. 'We won't be there by evening at this rate. All the bees'll be back in their hives.'

'...Four thousand eight hundwed and sixty. I can't go any faster. Four thousand eight hundwed and fifty-nine,' returned the caterpillar, inching back into step.

Hand on hips, Marcel stood waiting for the insect to catch up. 'And what do you keep counting backward for?' he asked, drawing the other arm across his pearling brow now that the heat from his exertions had caught up with him.

'To measure my step, Marcel. What do you expect? Four thousand eight hundwed and fifty-eight. See, when I get to zero, it means it's time to stop and snuggle into a comfy place before the changes start.'

'Ah, you mean metamorphosis,' said Marcel as a soft breeze ruffled through the grass tips. On his instinctive association of *changes* with *metamorphosis*, an appalling thought darted through his mind. When the gallfly spoke about changes, could she too have really meant metamorphosis?

The inchworm, meanwhile, had halted mid-step to lovingly sample the warm afternoon air with his antennae.

'Mmm, hey, Marcel, we can't be far fwom the first flowers!'

'How do you know?' asked Marcel, still with a tang of anxiety in his mouth.

'You can taste it in the air; the smell of pollen's getting stronger. Go on; take a good whiff. I detect daisy with a taint of buttercup,' said the inchworm, bobbing down and up again to feel it whiz through his body. 'Mmmmmm, buttercup's quite rare, you know, in a field where daisies grow,' he said.

Marcel, in turn, dipped his nose into a stream of breeze, and sure enough was rewarded with the sweetest smell. He instantly felt a hollow in his belly and a new craving.

'Mmmm, wow, that's gorgeous!'

'Hey, hey, and that's just for starters, Marcel. They say dandelion nectar is like a kiss from Ma Nature herself. And woyal jelly, oh, let me tell you about woyal jelly. They say it's like the sun melting in your mouth and twickling ever so sweetly thwough your whole body! Four thousand eight hundwed and fifty-two.'

'How far off are we from the flowers, Brimstone?' asked Marcel, more eager than ever to get on.

'No more than a hundwed strides, I'd say.'

'A hundred of your strides...that's...that can't be no more than three meters. Come on, Brim, get your running shoes on!' The boy clapped, and with the insect having made up ground, he resumed his course through the grassy jungle. *I'll take some refreshment myself,* he thought, now that his belly had been given the scent of buttercup nectar to rumble over. So he forged ahead, as much fuelled by the new craving as by the prospective of finding a bee to talk to.

But no more than ten paces later, alerted by gratifying outbursts in his ear, Marcel cast an eye back over his shoulder only to find the inchworm greedily tucking into another leafy snack, this time some clover.

'Mmm, oh, so delicious, mmmmm, oh weally, too much.'

'It's no time to be stopping now, Brimstone,' called Marcel, this time with a pinch of exasperation.

'I am sorry! Marcels might be equipped to live on fwesh air but inchworms aren't! And it's not my fault that I have to keep stopping for a bite, coz if I didn't, I'd whither like a parched flower, and then where would you be for a guide for your bees and woyal jelly?' said the inchworm quite unperturbed and with his mouth half full. 'Mmm, oh, this is so, so delicioso. See, that's another one of Ma Nature's little quirks, Marcel. I have to eat thousands of times my own weight from my first step to my last if I want to take off all light and fluttewy into the sky one day.'

'Well, can't you at least munch and march at the same time?' asked Marcel, becoming increasingly irritated.

'Inchworms don't munch an' march at the same time; inchworms are monofunctional. We like to concentrate on getting things wight the first time—saves time in the end—and life's too short to go wound wasting it. See, if I'm munching, how can I be thinking about the woute ahead, not to mention the commotion it makes inside your head!'

But Marcel was anxious to get on. Time was short enough without being weighed down by a dumb caterpillar's bottomless belly (not to mention his own, which was feeling pretty slim). 'Look, Brim, I can't just stand around waiting for you to catch up,' he said with a shrug of the shoulders. 'We'll have to call our deal off. I've really got to be making tracks.'

'But we shook on it.'

'Sorry, Brim.'

'And who's gonna be your guide then?' asked the inchworm, rumbling his short legs on the ground.

'I've never needed one before. I can get by on my own. Thank you, Brim.'

'But you're forgetting that there's spiders, birds, snakes, and—'

'Look, it's been interesting talking to you, but now I've got to get on. Good-bye,' said Marcel with finality, leaving the inchworm calling out more reasons why Marcel needed a guide.

'And there's lizards, poison leaves, killer plants, and gwasshoppers.'

But Marcel had already turned back, had his head down, and was powering his way through the great tufts of grass that towered over his head. *So much for loyal services* was the train of thought he followed to help him smother the pang of guilt at leaving his new comrade behind.

After a good deal of weaving, some hacking with a stick made from a twig, and a fair lot of scrambling on hands and knees, Marcel at last burst out of the thicket into a dazzling clearing of hard, flat, sunbaked earth. The boy paused, hands on knees, to catch his breath, glad to feel the firm ground beneath his shoe leather again. The sweet smells he had earlier sniffed now wafted into his nostrils. On looking up, some twenty paces across the clearing, he saw a towering buttercup and a host of dandelion stalks that reached into the deep-blue sky, each one topped with a yellow crown. All, that is, except one, which was coiffed with a feathery nimbus formed of beautifully luminous seeds. 'Who'd have thought I'd be standing in awe at the sight of dandelions one day!' Marcel mused.

The very next instant, he was shaken back into his present predicament by a low drone that quickly grew into a loud buzz. Recalling the inchworm's words of caution, he dived back into the undergrowth for cover, as the sharp shadow of a bee met that of a dandelion flower on the clayey ground of the clearing.

How on earth do I approach a bee? he wondered, squatting in the tall grass. *Should I call out? Or should I buzz something? But then how will I know what I'm buzzing? Might be an insult for all I know.* However, before he could make up his mind, the bee was off again. 'Blast it,' he said, swatting a spec of dust. 'If only the bloody inchworm didn't have a bottomless pit for a stomach, he'd still be with me!'

At that moment, another bee came and settled on another flower, and this time, pricked by his own failure to communicate, the boy jumped out into the sunny glade, waving his arms. 'Hey, bee, up there!' he hollered, but again barely had the bee settled than it was off again, without so much as a wiggle of an antenna at the strange creature doing a funny jig below.

On top of his frustration, his stomach was beginning to growl its discontent, and he could feel his strength beginning to drain away. So he approached the thinnest bristly dandelion stalk and began to shin his way up to the canopy of flower heads. *This way, I'll be killing two birds with one stone*, he thought as he strived to heave himself closer to the top. *I'll be close enough to attract the attention of the next bee that comes, and I'll be able to help myself to some refreshment.*

He was within arm's length of the yellow petals and hoping the pollen tasted as good as it smelled. But the mere thought of refreshment had sapped some of his remaining energy. Before he could refocus his thoughts on the task at hand, the faint breeze that made the dandelion stalk sway slightly was enough to relieve him of the last dregs of his force, the same force that had been so extraordinarily great during his intrepid rescue of the gallfly. Strain as he would, his arms were losing their grasping power. He found himself unable to prevent his inexorable slide back down the stalk, which was now covered in a liquid substance that the shinning had caused the plant to secrete.

On hitting the ground, the impetus made him fall plumb on his rump, which in turn puffed up a cloud of dust, making his already parched throat rasp as he spluttered his annoyance. There came another distant droning from overhead, and despite his setback, recalling the gallfly's last words, he mustered all his strength in an attempt to shin up another flower stalk, the previous one being too slippery. Only this time, the stalk being wider than the first, he was unable to wrap his arms and legs around it sufficiently to get a good grip. Before long, he was puffing up another cloud of dust, as the buzzing above grew fainter and faded away.

Exhausted from his exertion and embittered by his rotten performance, he gave the stalk a kick before letting himself fall flat on his back in a pool of sunshine. 'I can't go on. If only I could get some refreshment,' he said to himself faint-heartedly and so worn out that he lacked the force of mind to focus on a solution.

But then, against the backdrop of the summer sky, Marcel perceived tiny golden drops spill from the dandelion flower high above him. They tumbled softly down in a shaft of sunshine. Sitting up, he managed to catch two of them. They turned out to be pollen flakes that in his hand now were comparable to the size of wild plums. He kicked the stem again, and again pollen tumbled down. He instinctively brought the bright yellow crystal puffs to his nose—smells good—then to his tongue—tastes good—and finally popped one into his mouth. 'Wow, that's delicious, sweet as...as caramel and lighter than marshmallow,' he mused. Chewing down one pollen drop after another, he could gradually feel every muscle in every limb being revived, as if by magic, and every neuron in his head regaining its full charge.

Pretty soon, a metamorphosed Marcel sprang to his feet with a brainwave. 'Why didn't I think of it before?' he cried out, then undid his buckle, slipped off his belt, and looped it round another thick stalk so as to extend his hold.

With renewed strength and raised spirits, he began hoisting himself up the stem, this time that of a buttercup, as smart as any Canadian lumberjack. He was soon past the first embranchment at a breath-taking thirty-something centimeters aboveground.

For a person under two centimeters tall, at this height the slip of a hand could lead to disaster, and this time there would be no puffball to break his fall. Yet disaster did come in the form of a sudden flurry that whirled into the clearing and bowled into the buttercup, making it sway. When it hit, Marcel was in mid-hoist, and one end of his belt snatched tantalizingly from his hand. As he fell backward, he instinctively wrapped his legs around the stalk. In a desperate effort to keep from plummeting to the ground, he reached out his hands above and behind his head. If the law of gravity is anything to go by, his hands ought to have bounded off the surface of the buttercup stalk and continued their downward course toward the ground. But they did not. Instead, they stuck firm! The extent of the abrupt halt of his momentum caused his legs to follow through past his head, bringing him back to the upright position. Recovering from his unconventional back flip, Marcel carefully placed one hand after the other, up and down the stem, as the notion of his newfound suction power sunk in.

'Yahoo, this is fantastic,' he yelped, now scurrying up and down the stem like a tree frog spreading his digits for even better adhesion. *Incredible. If this is what pollen does, what can royal jelly do?* he thought, and then he scampered down to fetch his belt, which had fallen astride the lower embranchment. He did not realize for the moment that he had in fact undergone another physical mutation.

At last, wedging himself into the uppermost fork between two glossy buttercup heads, Marcel cast his gaze across the lush green sea of Graminae, with its crests and troughs, colored here and there by hillocks and pools of wild flowers—dandelion, daisy, marguerite, thistle, marigold, foxglove and ragwort—bowing their heads drowsily under the afternoon sun. The whole view was animated by a multitude of creatures of every color fluttering, flying, buzzing, and bounding across the vast meadow canopy in the busy airways of insect travel. *And to think only yesterday I was trampling over it all with old Malzac, without the slightest consideration*, thought Marcel. The boy then reached a hand up through the gap in a buttercup flower where a petal had fallen and managed to snap off a stamen. He popped the pollen-coated anther into his mouth, settled himself as best as he could in his fork, and scoured the vicinity for bees (though without the slightest idea of what to do if he saw one). For a blissful instant, he felt proud and as exhilarated as any jungle adventurer should now that his persistent efforts were paying off.

'A bee's bound to come bumblin' by here. There's a host of marguewites behind ya!' said an all-too-familiar voice. Marcel turned from his contemplation to see there, comfortably lounging in a half-eaten dandelion flower, none other than the inchworm. 'Even tastier than buttercup, marguewite, you know, you ought to twy some, though not as yummy as dandelion,' he said, munching away at some prized petals himself.

'Brimstone. How did *you* get here?' asked Marcel after the initial wonderment had passed.

'Oh, took a shortcut. Just as you went wunning off on your two long legs, I noticed a hollow that twavelled wight thwough the thicket you went hacking thwough, only a little to the left, over there, see?' said Brimstone, pointing with his stubby proleg. 'The unmistakeable hollow of a gwass snake's passage. Ever so useful for getting awound, you know. They make twavel so much easier, gwass snakes do, pwovided of course you don't come nose to nose with one!'

'How come *I* didn't notice the passage?'

'You wouldn't, would ya? Not with your head down and your legs plowing forward like there was no tomowwow. You gotta come up for air sometimes, you know, look awound a bit, might save you time and *energy* in the long wun,' said the inchworm, nonchalantly spilling some pollen over the brim of the flower with a knowing glance. Marcel peered down at the stalk of the dandelion that the inchworm occupied and recognized the foot of the stalk where not so long ago his dejected spirits had been raised by falling pollen flakes.

'You mean you've been spying!' said the boy, but his indignation was checked by a low, buzzing drone, and a blithe bee in handsome livery came to land on a marguerite right in front of him.

5

The Bee and the Rhino

Gripping hold with its claws, the bee drew its snout into the domed center of the flower to sup up the remaining nectar. This gave Marcel plenty of time to admire the slender, plumose body of the fine specimen. But then an incessant 'Psss' snapped him out of his contemplation.

'Go on, say something then!' urged Brimstone. 'Let's see if you can talk to bees!'

Marcel cleared his throat assertively as much to bolster his courage as to prepare his larynx for speech. 'Ke ke-her, hello there,' he called without taking his eye off the lethal dart at the point of the bee's abdomen. But the bee pulled out its snout, combed back the pollen drops stuck to its body into a compact pile behind its hind tibia, and flew on farther afield.

'You certainly know how to talk to bees!' chaffed Brim. 'Look out, here comes another.' The bee in question landed with the same dexterity as the first and drew its body headfirst into the middle of the flower, this time a dandelion.

'Hello there,' called Marcel, holding onto the buttercup stem with one hand and waving his stamen-lollypop with the other. But the bee didn't so much as give a glance in the boy's direction before it, too, pulled out its trunk and hit the airways.

'You're certainly turning out to be a charmer with the dames, Marcel! Hah, I hope you've better luck with marcelettes!' teased Brimstone, bending over backward with laughter.

'It's not my fault that they're as common as muck!'

'On the contwary, Marcel, bees are delicate cweatures, but they won't give you the time of day unless you know how to say hello pwoperly to them.'

'And how do you say 'hello' properly in bee talk then?'

'You say 'Hello' and give a little bow. They appweciate that, it flatters their ego, makes 'em feel a cut above the west,' said the inchworm, enacting a ceremonious bow on the rise of which he pulled a surprised face and shrieked, 'Watch out—bee behind!' Marcel ducked just before a plump-looking bee rounded the buttercups waveringly and made a wonky landing on the pollinated stigmas of a neighboring dandelion. She plunged her muzzle hungrily into the nectary then pulled it out again in disgust.

'Oh, typical. There's none left!' she said and proceeded to fondly lick her claws in consolation.

'Go on,' prompted Brimstone, two flowers back. 'And don't forget to bow.'

Marcel took a steady foothold, and with one hand firmly stuck on the stalk, he said, 'Hello, Mrs. Bee,' and made as low a bow as any marcel could while standing in the fork of a buttercup stem. 'I was wondering if you could tell me where I might find some freshly made royal jelly,' he continued in his best, most educated voice. The bee interrupted her licking, lifted her head, and said in a plummy voice, 'Oh, hello. Sorry, but do speak up; all this buzzing around's left me head ringing.'

'I said I was wondering, Mrs. Bee, if you'd be so kind as to tell us the way to some fresh royal jelly,' reiterated the boy, glad for the attention.

'Oh, I can't do that. It's forbidden, and it's Miss, not Mrs., if you please. You are a strange creature. Now, if you don't mind, I've my stockings needing filling, and the sun stands still for no creature!' replied the bee, grooming her wings in preparation for liftoff.

'Wait, Miss Bee, please don't fly off yet,' implored Marcel and turned desperately to his discharged guide. 'Brimstone, say something and I'll reinstate you as my guide.'

'I don't know about that. You already broke your word once. I don't know if I can believe you now.'

'You can believe me. All right, I was wrong. Please give me another chance; I promise I won't go back on my word again. Come on, Brimstone, be my guide, please.'

'Hmmm, your *iwwevocable* guide then.'

'Yes, yes, my irrevocable guide,' said Marcel. With a winning grin, Brimstone immediately turned toward the bee.

'Good day to you, pwetty bee,' he said. He bowed ceremoniously without losing sight of her, which meant that his body took on the shape of an S. 'Oh, dear, if you don't mind me saying,' he continued with empathy, 'you're pwetty thin on pollen today.'

'That's because the others keep getting their noses in first! One must make do,' replied the perceptibly sensitive bee standing high and mighty on her hind legs.

'With respect, Miss Bee, what you've got don't smell as pwemium as it ought neither for one such as your noble self!' said the inchworm brimming with confidence after sensing the bee's weak spot.

'All I ever get is the stodgy leftovers. I've a good mind to report the unfair competition to Her Majesty. For I, you see, have been burdened with an insatiable appetite from birth. By consequence I am obliged to pull a lot more weight around than my counterparts,' said the bee, defending her foible in her plummy, highbrow accent.

'Then I think we can come to an equitable awwangement, Miss Bee. Listen, I can tell you where to find some fweshly blooming sunflowers, just bwimming with nectar. The first of the season, Miss Bee, and plenty to fill your baskets a thousand times over and still have enough left over for a well-earned indulgence if the fancy takes you.'

'I say, sunflowers already, no one's discovered any of those yet. I'd be the talk of the colony. I'll show 'em who's a tubby bee with no sense of direction!' proclaimed the tubby bee in question, warming both to the prospect of glory and nourishing her foible.

'All you have to do is tell us where your nest is then, and I'll tell you where the flowers are,' said the inchworm while the idea was still hot in the bee's bonnet and belly. But the bee's blithe expression turned suddenly sour, as if her favorite dish was being taken away from under her very nose.

'Oh, dear, I can't tell you that; it's forbidden to tell colony details to strangers, especially since sightings of giant hornets.'

'We hardly look like hornets, do we? But don't fwet, Miss Bee, I've thought about that for you. See, you can't *tell* us, but you can *show* us, and showing isn't telling, is it?' said Brimstone brightly.

'No, showing is definitely not telling,' seconded Marcel, standing in his buttercup fork between the flowers where the insects had settled. 'Telling is saying, and showing is definitely not saying.'

Prompted by the scarcity of her day's takings, the bee visibly shed a clement light of thought on the subject. 'That's true. I can't say you're wrong.' But then another false note rumpled her bee-ish brow and interrupted her train of thought before it could reach a satisfactory conclusion (satisfactory, that is, for the inchworm and the boy). 'But why are you so interested in the nest in the first place? Inchworms don't have honey, do they?' she said.

'Well, it's for me. See, I'm supposed to meet my fiancée under the tree where royal jelly is produced,' said Marcel softening his voice in an attempt to pluck the heartstrings of the spinster. But the spinster simply began nonchalantly combing her body for pollen drops.

'Just think, budding sunflowers fwesh as the new day's dew and nectar warmed in the sun,' piped the inchworm, who knew better where the bee's heartstrings lay.

'Oh, Master Inchworm, you certainly know how to talk to a bee; I grant you that,' said the bee and licked her palps again at the mere notion of sunflower nectar. 'All right then, I'll show you. I'll do a dance for you, but I want to see the flowers first, with all due respect.'

Brimstone recoiled as if struck by a sudden affliction. 'We are cweatures of honor, Miss Bee. You'll have to take our word for it,' he argued.

'No doubt you are, but I only take what I can see. I promise, as soon as I've seen the flowers with my own eyes, I shall come straight back and dance the way to the nest for you,' insisted the bee with a note of condescendence and totally unmoved by the inchworm's continuing indignation.

Marcel leaned toward the inchworm, and directing his hoarse whisper with a cupped hand, he said, 'Don't tell her. She might not come back, and we'll have lost our bargaining power.'

In an equal whisper, Brimstone hushed back, 'Don't wowwy, Marcel, bees might be clanny and mannered with it, but one thing I will say for 'em is they don't tell lies.' Then, clearing his throat, he spoke up for the bee, who had been taking advantage of the interlude to coquettishly wax her antennae. 'All wight, you got a deal, but pwomise you'll come back quick. The marcel here is despewate to find his mate. His nuptial season starts soon!'

So it was agreed that the bee would first visit the flowers and, without so much as a dip in a nectary, would bumble back and do a dance to indicate where the nest was located. She took to the air on a slight breeze amid the smell of freshly cut grass and a score of dandelion seeds blown from a flower a little farther on.

'Please, be quick, Miss Bee,' Marcel called as she buzzed over the plant he was perched in. This was a big mistake. Being of a rather distracted disposition, the bee swiveled her head back with her reply, so deviating the course of her flight.

'Don't tell anyone else about the—'

'Look out!' cried Marcel, but it was too late. Before the poor bee could finish her sentence, she was hit head-on by a rhinoceros beetle cruising at over twenty kilometers per hour.

Upon impact, the two crumpled creatures plummeted to the ground.

'Ahh, can't you learn to fly straight, fatty!' was all Marcel heard the one-horned beetle growl before it passed out.

'Oh, dear, I'm stuck. My thorax is locked—help!' cried the bee, but her continued plea was now drowned out by an awful rhythmic swishing noise and the heavy thud of hooves. Marcel, quick as a flash, scurried as far up as he could to the crest of the buttercup only to see his fears confirmed.

'It's old Malzac with his ox and mower, cutting the grass. The bee's exactly in his path! Come on, Brim, we've got to save her!'

The inchworm, who had reached over to a neighboring plant, was munching a piece of leaf and nonchalantly raised his head and said, 'Oh, don't wowwy, Marcel; there's plenty more bees in the field. As long as the sun will shine and flowers bloom, there's bound to be bees awound,' he said. 'Hah, else half the plants awound 'ere would never see the light of day.'

'But we can't just leave her there. Come on!'

'You'll never get there in time, Marcel,' said Brim, but Marcel had already caught hold of the stem of a drifting dandelion seed in midair and was floating down to the ground with his legs swinging to and fro to steer himself toward the wounded bee. The inchworm was left balancing the odds as to whether following Marcel to royal jelly would lead to success or suicide, and the odds at the moment seemed pretty much in favor of the latter, he concluded.

The boy hit the ground and was racing over the flattened grass blades through the grass snake passage on the other side of which he knew the bee lay agonizing.

6

Somewhere Along the Squirrel Run

The terrifying sound of the mower pounded louder and louder. At last he reached the collision zone where the two injured creatures lay motionless. He first approached the bee, who had passed out. But push and tug as he would, for the life of him, the plump creature just would not budge. Concentrating his efforts, he again put his head down, grit his teeth, and gave the honeybee another pull with all his might, and this time the bee began to move.

'We'll never...make it...in time...out of the monster's...path,' called a voice between heaving grunts. On looking up, Marcel saw the reason of his newfound strength. 'No use dwagging her; her claws keep catching!' called the inchworm, who stopped pushing at a spot where the earth stepped down a centimeter and lined himself up against the bee's flank in the dip in the ground. 'Hook her on,' he shouted, barely making himself heard above the growing clamor. No sooner said than Marcel was sliding the tubby bee onto the inchworm's back and hooking her tarsal claws on between the caterpillar's segments so she wouldn't roll off. 'Now, you wun on!' cried Brimstone. But instead, the boy jumped over to the rhinoceros beetle and pulled at its horn. With the jerk, the creature raised a groggy head as the ground trembled on the approach of the hooves of the ox.

'We're cooked,' yelled Brim, as the breath of the great snorting animal came upon them. 'Leave us, Marcel. Wun on while you still can! This is our fate; it needn't be yours!'

'No, Brim, I'm not letting you down again,' bellowed Marcel, pointing to a pothole no larger than a two-franc piece that had opened up in the earth between the great hooves. 'It's our only chance!'

'Oh, no, not the tunnel, I won't go,' blurted the rhinoceros beetle deliriously as Marcel tugged it forward with all his might amid the swirling tornado caused by the approaching blades. Seconds later the four creatures—a bee on the back of an inchworm and a groggy rhinoceros beetle being steered by a marcel—were bundling down the hole into an underground gallery as the insatiable grass eater with its terrifying blades screamed by scything the tall grass not four inches above their heads. The ceiling shook and the earth crumbled from the gallery walls, but they were safe, and the awful din was soon a distant rumbling.

'You all right, Brimstone?' said Marcel, picking himself up.

'None the worse for wear, considewing,' said the inchworm, who had shed his load in the tumble.

'Oh, my back, oh, where am I?' wailed the bee, coming round. She was lying upside down with her six feet in the air.

'You're safe now, Miss Bee. You had an accident.'

'Urgh, what are you?' exclaimed the bee, pulling a revolted face.

'That's the marcel; he saved you. And I'm the inchworm. We had a deal—wemember?'

'A deal?' said the bewildered bee. 'I don't remember anything of the sort.'

'You were to show us where the woyal jelly is kept,' said Brimstone, conveniently omitting the first part of the deal.

'Royal jelly? Never heard of such a thing!' said the bee, endeavoring to remain dignified in spite of her indelicate position. Marcel and the inchworm looked at one another in dismay.

'Don't tell me she's gone and lost her memowy,' said the inchworm.

'Miss Bee, do you remember where you live?' Marcel asked gravely.

'In a bee nest, do you have any more silly questions?'

'But exactly where do you live?'

'No use trying to trick me into telling you either,' said the bee still clinging to her dignity.

'What you really mean is that you can't remember, can you?' said Marcel sympathetically.

'I couldn't show you even if I wanted to, not down here, not without the sun.' With that, the realization of her predicament dawned on her, her antennae began to tremble, and she began to sob.

'I knew it, she *has* gone and lost her memowy!' said the inchworm.

'No, she's just lost her bearings. Don't cry, Miss Bee,' said Marcel, trying to be compassionate.

'What do you expect me to do? I don't know where I am, I don't know where I'm from, I'm hungry, and I can't even reach my own shopping baskets!' lamented the ailing bee. Then pulling herself together, she continued in a more dignified tone. 'You may as well eat me now; I only ask you not to linger.'

Indeed, taking advantage of the bee's forced immobility and her being illuminated by the beam of light streaming in from the aperture above, Marcel was now drawing an admiring eye over her anatomy. He was considering her fine "engineering" while perusing the undercarriage of the exoskeleton and the "ball joints" where the legs joined the thorax. *There's an idea for my steering column,* he thought to himself as his gaze focused on a point where the thorax met the abdomen.

'Please get on with it. It's cruel to let one suffer. I'm ready to meet Mother Nature now.'

'Sorry, Miss Bee, I don't eat bees, but I think I can put you out of your misery. Now, just think of something nice. I promise I won't be a sec.'

'Nice, like what?'

'Like sunflowers bwimming with nectar warmed to a tee in the afternoon sun,' piped in the inchworm. The bee's large faceted eyes glazed over with the mere evocation of her favorite nectar, while Marcel adroitly took a firm grasp of the legs on the third segment of the thorax and gave them a sharp, strong yank. There was a clean click, closely followed by a yelp, and the dislocated thorax was put back into place.

'Try and get to your feet now,' said Marcel. With the sudden relief from her suffering, the bee forgot all about being eaten and flipped herself joyously back onto her tarsi.

'I say, it doesn't hurt!' she trilled, wagging her abdomen.

'Amazing!' cried Brimstone proudly.

'Look, I can crawl!'

'Didn't tell you, did I? The marcel's a genius! I personally spotted it the first time I saw him, you know. We've been fwiends ever since; I'm his personal guide, you know!' said the inchworm to the bee in quite a condescending sort of way.

'You might not be able to fly immediately, though, Miss Bee. Better give it time to heal properly,' said Marcel, recalling the time he put his collarbone out after falling from the pit in the oak tree.

'Oh, we'll soon see about that,' said the bee. But buzz as she would, her wings seemed out of sync with each other, and instead of going up to the aperture, she went round and round on the ground like a mad dog chasing its tail.

From the shadows there came a movement and some grunting. 'Where the boggin' bluebells am I? This the tunnel to heaven, is it?' said the gruff voice of the rhinoceros beetle, who was coming back to his senses.

'No, we've just pulled you in here out of danger,' said Brim.

'Oh, thank boggin' goodness. And what's fatso bumbling about like a blue-arsed fly for? Tell her to stop before she knocks someone else out, boggin' public danger, she is, going round wasting critters' precious time!' he groused. 'You ought to conduct her back to her nest and have her nursing grubs for the rest of her days!'

'Thanks for the suggestion, Rhinoceros. We would take her back if we could, but she's lost her bearings; she doesn't know where her nest is!' said Marcel.

'Well, *I* do, and so should every winged critter in the neighborhood. The boggin' maids are noisy enough!' said the rhinoceros. 'Anyway, I heard you talking earlier. You're after royal jelly, ain't ya?'

'Well, yes, I need some to grow to full human-size,' said Marcel frankly. For some reason, judging he could trust the gruff and forthright creature, the boy gave him a quick rundown of his predicament.

'I'll help ya get to the nest,' said the rhino spontaneously. 'Long as I get my share of royal jelly, mind. They say it extends your life; I might live as long as the queen. See, I ain't ready for ol' Ma Nature's light yet,' said the beetle with a snort. Marcel agreed, and the rhino said, 'The bee nest is in the lime tree along the squirrel run.'

After a short pause for thought, Marcel declared: 'I know where that is. Squirrels run from the walnut trees behind the pigeon house to the cedar tree by skipping through the lime tree in front of the dining room.'

'Then that's where we'll find the fwesh woyal jelly!' exalted Brimstone, beating his tail against the floor. 'I told you I'd find it for you!'

'Ah, boggin' bluebells!' said the rhinoceros, straining on his hind legs as if to lift off. 'Look, can't get me wings open. She must have boggin' well jammed me casings in the crash.'

However, their jubilation and the rhino's protests were short-lived. Overhead, the ceiling began to crumble, the rhythmic raucous of pounding hooves and swishing blades once again grew deafening. The grass-eating monster was coming back for afters. The four creatures scampered for cover as an ox hoof hit the pothole above, bunching up the earth around it, so blocking it off completely. The scything convoy, led by Malzac the gardener, soon passed on, but the way out was sealed.

7
A Disused Tunnel

'Looks like you won't be needing your wings just yet, Rhinoceros,' said Marcel, picking himself up again from the clayey earth. 'But no panic,' he continued, as much for himself as for the others. 'There's light coming in from somewhere; there must be another exit point ahead. Come on, let's get going!'

Even if he had mentally accepted his surreal quest, you would have to admit, the whole insect business did seem highly suspect to say the least. And who were his companions really? Could he really trust them? Yet there he was, there they were, in territory completely unknown to him, and there was no time for introspection. So after a few more gripes from the rhinoceros, with a resolute step forward, the intrepid young human waved to the company to follow his lead down the slightly sloping gradient of the gloomy winding tunnel. The faint light fed Marcel's eyesight just enough for him to pick up his feet over the woody roots that wound their way across the passage from one concave wall to the other and to dodge the odd grass root ends that dangled from the ceiling above.

At times, the gallery reminded him of the draughty loft of the tobacco barn to the back of the house of Villeneuve. It was there that he once pretended to Henriette that the coiling tobacco strings were hanging worms to make her cringe. Right now, it was his turn to cringe. But otherwise the path was conveniently flattened and smoothed. The fourteen feet (six + six + two) drummed on to the rhythmic scuff made by the inchworm amid the eerie sounds of the living earth around them. Here a thud-thudding, there a tap-tapping, there again a wrenching sound. And once again, Marcel was holding up a hand to halt the company and lend an ear.

'What we stoppin' for this time?' asked the rhinoceros.

'Shh, I thought I heard that tapping again,' Marcel whispered.

'That's hardly surprising; after all, it *is* the season for flowers to be growing, and this is where they all sprout from,' said the bee, encompassing the surrounding earth with a sweep of a limb. 'I expect the darling little things are trying to push themselves up,' she went on, moony-eyed at the mere thought of flowers.

'Do you know, wight above our 'eads, there's a lovely yellow ragwort?' observed Brim.

'How do you know?' asked Marcel.

'Those are the woots up there, dangling thwough the ceiling, see!'

'Well there's no leaves nor flowers down here, so you can stop licking your lips!' said the rhinoceros, bringing their gazes back down to earth, or rather, in it. 'If I were yous, I'd be asking myself who this tunnel belongs to, coz someone must have made it.'

'Hmm, it has a round aspect, and it is fairly smooth on all sides with scuffmarks on the walls. But there is no sign of footprints to give a clue, other than the ones we've left behind,' said Marcel thoughtfully.

'Can't be a vole's then; I'm weally glad about that!' said Brim, stopping for a quick nibble on a root that poked through the wall.

'So am I,' seconded the bee with a shudder.

'It must have been made by something cylindrical that leaves no footprints then.' said the rhinoceros knowingly.

An alarming thought suddenly shot through Brimstone's brain. 'Blimey, you mean it's a snake's!' The rhinoceros gave a glum nod.

'I s'pose on one hand, we can count ourselves lucky. Indirectly it has saved our lives,' said Marcel, trying to look on the bright side.

'And on the other, it's out of the beak and into the web,' groused the rhinoceros.

'Don't worry; there's not much chance of bumping into a snake down here. Look, the tunnel's been disused for ages, probably since last winter. We wouldn't be stumbling on roots otherwise, would we? Come on, the light's getting stronger ahead,' said Marcel.

Thirty paces later, the company huddled at a left-hand bend in the tunnel where a narrower gallery forked off to the right through an opening in the wall. This is where the faint light of day was filtering through and offered an eye-nourishing contrast to the tunnel, which meandered on into utter darkness.

'This is the way. Can't be far now, and then we're out!' said Marcel, pointing to the gallery entrance.

'I wouldn't say it exactly smells inviting in there,' said the inchworm with a dubious quiver.

'Neither would I,' seconded the bee with a shudder of the abdomen. 'It smells positively creepy.'

'I don't see we've got much choice,' said Marcel with a glance from the faintly glowing gallery to the chilling darkness of the tunnel. 'That way you wouldn't see the tip of your nose let alone where you're putting your feet!'

'At least the air is better there, though,' said the bee. 'But if you must go that way, then if you don't mind, I'd rather stay behind. I couldn't bear the thought of…of that hideous odor clinging to me. At least here, it's clean-ish.'

Although the boy lacked the insects' keen olfactory organ to detect any foulness in the air, he did sense there was something more than just the smell behind the bee's unexpected refusal to proceed. But as he was about to string his thoughts into words, the rhinoceros lifted his massive horned head and in his gruff voice said, 'What she means is that the smell brings out the jitters in her belly.'

'The jitters?'

'Yes, the jitters make you want to keep away fwom danger. Otherwise none of us would be able to accomplish our mission in life,' said the inchworm.

'Only, some of us get them more often than others,' said the bee.

'And the ones that gets 'em most are called jitterbellies,' said the rhinoceros.

'I admit I am a jitter-belly, but it's hardly my fault if I get more jitters than most, is it? And I might add, my refined condition makes them all the more unbearable.'

'But what's giving you the jitters, Miss Bee? I can't smell anything,' said Marcel.

'You wouldn't; you haven't got any antennas!' replied the bee.

Marcel moved his head closer to the entrance and sniffed the air. 'Now you mention it, there *is* a kind of tangy smell.'

'That tangy smell means wasps!' said the rhinoceros, and the bee gave a double shudder of the abdomen at the mere evocation.

'Wasps? You mean you're afraid of wasps, Miss Bee? There's really no need to be. That gallery is probably as disused as this snake tunnel,' said Marcel in an attempt to make a small thing of the bee's phobia. 'You can't be scared of just a smell. I mean, what do you usually do if you smell a wasp near your favorite flowers?'

'I fly the other way, of course!'

'And miss out!'

'Yes, but I try not to think about it; otherwise, I get angry with myself.'

'Listen, Miss Bee, sometimes your fears come to test you. The good news is that if you stand up to them, they'll help make your life better. Think of this one as a chance to beat off those wasp jitters. Think of the delicious nectar you'll be able to sup up if you do, instead of flying the other way just because you get a whiff of a wasp.'

'No, no, I think I'll just wait here 'til Mother Nature's light dawns on me and leads me through the tunnel to the next world.'

'But you won't finish your mission,' protested Marcel.

'If that's my fate, then so be it,' said the bee resignedly.

'But the fact remains, Miss Bee, you're the only one with a reserve of food. Without it I'd be surprised if we got twenty paces into that gallery, let alone back into the fresh air!' said Marcel, shrewdly playing on the bee's innate sense of loyalty.

'That's true,' seconded the rhinoceros with a slow nod of his massive head.

'Now that you mention it, I'm feeling all weak myself,' said the inchworm, eyeing up the bulging pollen baskets on the bee's hind legs.

'I say, that's unfair!'

'Look, Miss Bee, no one else has baskets to carry your harvest in. If you don't take up your courage in your own hands, or rather your tarsi, you'll be as good as stabbing us in the backs with your dart!'

The bee looked from one to the other of her companions and beseeched, 'But the smell, it's just too insufferable!'

'All right, if I take away the smell, you'll come with us, right?' urged Marcel.

'Think of the joys of supping up nectar once you're out in the sun again,' prompted the inchworm, licking his lips himself.

'Well I, I...' stammered the bee, out of argumentative substance, while Marcel surreptitiously brought out a phial of Rêve d'Ossian perfume from his inner jacket pocket. He ceremoniously untwisted the top.

'This is a special potion. It's capable of chasing away the most unpleasant odors from your sniffing range,' he said, wafting the bottle beneath his own nose before holding it under the bee's antennae.

'I say, that's delicious,' she said, while Marcel proceeded in dabbing his handkerchief over the top of the bottle, then (with permission) he rubbed the bee's antennae.

'You'll see, it works wonders, Miss Bee.' And sure enough, her reservations soon dissipated.

'Oh, do please call me Bea,' she said, curling her antennae into arabesques. 'Mmmm, I can smell jasmine, I can smell wild rose, I can smell woodbine, lavender... Oh, I feel better already!'

Now armed with Marcel's magic scent, she at last agreed to wait another day for Mother Nature's light to beam her up to the place where insects go after life. To get their motors ticking again, she invited each of the company to pick a pollen drop or three from her golden stacks.

'Allow me to compliment you, Miss Bea, on your deft rolling!' said Brimstone, only too glad for the change from weed root.

And so the four creatures resumed their step and entered the orifice of the gallery one by one. Marcel took the lead, followed by Brimstone, and then came Miss Bea, with the rhinoceros closing up the rear.

By and by, the pungent smell sharply intensified until the tunnel became stifling, and Marcel himself was obliged to hold his handkerchief over his nose. With the exception of the odd grunt from the rhinoceros, the motley train crept up and round without dropping a sound for fear of interrupting the noises of scraping and gnawing that grew louder with every step further into the dreaded passageway. Now the presence of wasps somewhere up ahead was undeniable. But the darkness growing paler coaxed the company to steadfastly put one foot before the other until very soon they saw the source of light not ten paces ahead.

On their approach, the bee gave a horrified gasp. Her abdomen shuddered half a dozen times before she was able to bring it under control.

'Pull yourself together, dame!' belched the rhino under his breath. 'You'll start buzzing next, and we'll have the whole boggin' wasp nest on top of us!'

'Actually,' said Brimstone, gazing up in awe toward the light, 'it *is* on top of us!' All eyes met the underground wasp nest suspended above their heads in the middle of the cavern. All eyes, that is, except the bee's, which were looking across the clearing to the left.

'Oh, oh, oh, horrible, horrible,' she whimpered.

'What is it, Bea?' said Marcel.

The rhinoceros took a few paces forward under the nest. He bowed his great head dolefully and said, 'Dead bees. At least what's left of 'em.'

Marcel, on joining him, could now clearly make out the morbid litter of bee heads and decapitated bodies scattered about the floor directly under the entrance of the nest.

Suddenly there was a deep, stomach-churning hum and a desperate cry. A wasp must have entered through the hole in the ground above and was approaching the entrance of the nest located further down near the bottom. The company dived behind a mound of earth just as an enormous guard burst out of the entrance and waited on the edge.

'Crikey, that's not a wasp,' whispered Marcel, 'that's a giant hornet!'

In the next instant, the returning orange-faced predator appeared at the entrance, holding a bee captive in its mandibles. The guard touched feelers and said, 'Cute, where d'ya find her?'

'Near the pond, sir.'

'And how many's that today?'

'Thirty-eight.'

'Well, number thirty-eight,' said the guard to the bee, 'how would you like to join your sisters?'

'No, no, let me go,' cried the bee, swiveling her head down at the awful mass of corpses.

'All right. Just say where your nest is, and you can go free.'

'No, no, I will never tell,' said the brave bee and spat at the guard.

'Give her a little squeeze, Zid, just in case she's got more sense than the others.' The awesome exterminator slowly tightened its grasp around the bee's abdomen. The bee yelped in agony.

'No, I won't talk...I won't,' she cried, trying in vain to jab the hornet with her dart.

'Nope? Oh, well, they're all the same. Finish her off!'

Marcel, unable to stand it anymore, jumped up with a raised fist. But before he could expulse his indignation, a sudden jerk of the head from the rhinoceros sent him bowling back on his butt. Meanwhile the ferocious beast gave a satisfying sigh on bringing its mandibles effortlessly together. The bee's head and body dropped to the heap in two separate parts.

'Keep sniffing round. There's another couple of hours harvesting time yet; their nest can't be far off. The siblings are crying out for more bee grub, and they don't grow on trees!' said the guard.

Again Marcel jumped up, but it was the voice of Miss Bea that called out. 'Assassins!' Marcel and Rhino had to literally wrestle her back down and bring her to her senses.

'What was that?' responded the guard. 'You sure you killed that last bee?'

'I sectioned it at its waist!'

'Hmmm, there's a strange smell coming from somewhere,' said the guard, twitching its antennae. 'Go see just in case, we can't have any of 'em getting back with word to their queen.'

'But—'

'Go check; that's an order!'

The killer hornet hovered a second above the ground, scattering dust before settling in front of the pile of decapitated bodies. It swiveled its head, twitched its feelers, and said, 'Something smells suspect down here. Lavender, rose, jasmine—that ain't right!' Then it bounded toward the mound where Marcel and company had been hiding. 'There's been a bee here,' it said and zoomed in the trail of the scent across the clearing under the nest.

The small crew were shifting toward the gallery. Sensing the shadow of the enemy encroach, Marcel turned only to find a petrified Bea going into what can only be described as ground-winging. She suddenly went whizzing like a spinning top round and round across the floor, completely out of control until she spun straight into the hornet that was about to snap at the rhino's heels.

'Ah, there you are, fat little bee, come back here,' said the hornet, standing with its lacerating mandibles open wide to greet her as she came spinning back.

'Help, help!' cried the bee, unavoidably spinning toward the horrible deathtrap. The awesome predator lunged forward to encompass her. But the instant it did so, it found its right-hand mandible snagged.

'Hold it there, Rhino!' hollered Marcel, pulling his belt from around his waist while Brim inched in to knock the bee out of harm's reach with his tail. The hornet would have by now sliced through the bee, not to mention the inchworm, if the rhinoceros beetle had not hooked his horn underneath one mandible preventing it from meeting the other. In a tug of war between life and death, he held it with all his might. Without a thought for his own life, Marcel bounded to the rhino's side as the ferocious creature instinctively turned its head to bring its jaws together. The moment they were closed enough, Marcel managed to deftly loop his belt around them to prevent them from opening.

'Raaahhh, get it off!' roared the incensed hornet, beating its muzzled killing device from side to side, throwing Marcel and the rhino aside. The creature went into a blind fury dashing its muzzle against the wall to get rid of its tether. The next instant, in a moment of lucidity, it turned with its lethal dart poised. 'You're not getting away!' it hurled.

'We've had it now!' said Bea.

'Never say die!' cried Marcel. 'Now hold your breath!' And he swiped the killing jar cord from around his neck and cast it at the flank of the hornet. The jar smashed against the hard chitin near the hornet's spiracles where it took in air.

'Keep spinning, Bea!' shouted Marcel.

'I can't go on anymore; I can't!' called the bee, desperately dodging another jab of the dart. The awesome creature sprung into the air for a better angle of attack. It hovered above the bee, taking its time, poised for the kill.

'Excellent sport, I only wish it could last!' scoffed the hornet. But against all expectations, the creature suddenly froze in midair, and crashed to the ground in a crumpled heap. The ethyl acetate released from the killing jar had at last kicked in.

'Well, I be blowed,' declared the rhino amid cheers from Brim and Bea, while Marcel quickly and cautiously retrieved his belt. But there was no time for celebration.

'Come on, let's get out of here!' he hollered, beckoning the insects back through the gallery.

8

A Touch of the Jitters

'I must say it's nice to take in fresh air again!' said Bea, airing herself back in the spacious snake tunnel while giving out nourishment from her reserve.

'Huh, back to boggin' square one!' said the rhino.

'We'd have saved ourselves a lot of bother if we'd gone the other way in the first place!' said Brim.

'Oh, I don't regret our little excursion. Hah, I no longer fear wasps at all now that I've seen one! Now at least I can die a better bee,' rejoiced Bea and did a little jig in the relative freshness of the derelict snake tunnel.

'No one's going to die, Bea. We'll just have to figure out a way of breaking through the ceiling where we first fell in.'

'I say we're better off continuing further into the tunnel, Marcel. It smells of fwesh air down there; it must be coming fwom somewhere outside. And besides that, have you ever twied making a hole in a ceiling upside-down?'

'But there's no light that way; no light no way out, Brimstone. Surely you understand that!' said Marcel, becoming slightly prickled by the inchworm's insistence.

'No light don't necessarily mean no way out, Marcel. The way out might just be blocked off, like the ceiling,' said the rhinoceros. 'See, all us insects know the smell of fresh air from birth; it's what leads us to the Light. I remember the time I came of age and I 'ad to come up. It was pitch black all around, but I just followed the scent of fresh air. And the more I kicked and pushed and clawed my way toward it, the stronger it got, until at last I broke to the surface and found the Light of spring.'

'Here, here,' said Bea. 'Ones eyesight might detect things quicker, but you're always better off preferring your sense of smell in the end. For one thing, one can't see round corners, but you *can* smell what's round 'em.'

'And if there's one thing that stays constant in life for evewyone, it's the smell of fwesh air. And I'll bet you a belly full of pollen dwops that the tunnel will lead us out! Take my word, Marcel, as your iwwevocable guide. Can't ya smell it?'

'No, I can't.'

'Probably got grime in 'is feelers!' said the rhino.

'Marcel, I know how you feel,' said Bea meaningfully. 'Remember, I had the jitters, too. Call it feminine intuition if you like, but I think you're suffering from darkness jitters. And that's what's stopping you from smelling the fresh air. Instead you smell fear.'

Marcel bowed his head and after a moment's pause, he said, 'All right, I s'pose it is true I don't exactly love dark places, or rather what's in them.'

'Well, don't you think now's a good time to be cured?'

'No, Bea, I do not.'

'But you said yourself that trials come to help make us better, and if you succeed, you'll be able to move on to new horizons. Didn't *I* stand under a hornet nest?' said Bea, emphatically stamping a foot on the ground.

Was it the acceptance of his fear or the pang of hunger? At any rate, the boy suddenly felt an abnormal tingling sensation inside his organs and pins and needles coursing through his veins. Then a feeling that could be described as someone plowing furrows in his belly made him double over in spasms.

'Marcel, you all right?' said an anxious Bea after a short while.

'Yes, I'm okay now. It's passed; must be the smell,' he said. Yet he could not help thinking that he had felt the same faintness in his limbs and turmoil in his belly before, once at the foot of the dandelion stem and once underneath the oak tree.

'Here, take a pollen drop to settle yourself,' said Bea with a forced smile, matching that of the rhinoceros and the inchworm.

Marcel wolfed down the welcome nourishment. But then he almost brought it back up just as quickly with a hiccup of horror.

'Ah! My hand, God, look at my hand!' he gasped as he removed it from his mouth.

'And that ain't all,' said the rhinoceros.

'What d'you mean?'

'Wemember what the gallfly said, Marcel: "The more you find out about yourself, the more you'll change,"' recalled the inchworm to the letter.

A series of events shot through Marcel's mind: his miniaturization, his extraordinary strength on the spider's thread, his gripping powers. He stared down at the short bristles on the backs of his hands with disgust. Following his companions' gazes fixed toward his head, he said incredulously as he felt the chitinous bases of two short antennae, 'Ah! No, you mean...I'm turning into an insect?'

'It's not that bad, you know,' said the rhinoceros.

'I think they suit you fine,' said Bea.

'Oh, God, no! What about Monsieur Deforge, what about Henriette, what about Julia...and my scholarship?'

'We'll just have to get you to the woyal jelly quick then, won't we fellas?' said Brimstone, who was firmly seconded by Bea, and even the rhinoceros managed a grunt of consent.

'Yes, the royal jelly, before it's too late,' said Marcel, breathing more calmly. He realized that if all this was really happening, then he must keep his composure and think on his feet. 'But there must be some other way than through the tunnel, though.'

'Beats me what you're worried about,' said the rhino. 'There's less danger in darkness, because there's less creatures that thrives on it. Apart from snakes, voles, moles, and spiders...' Just as the rhinoceros said this, the bee was suddenly taken by another one of her funny turns.

'What's up, dame! Mention a spider, and she goes nutty!' said Rhino.

'But I'm not afraid of spiders!' trilled the bee, ground-winging around the place in spite of herself.

All of a sudden, a syncopated clamor arose from the gallery, and all eyes met with the most appalling sight. The huge hornet sprang forth and made a terrifying lunge in the midst of the company. Marcel dodged the hideous beast just in time, leaving it to crash to the ground where its antennae twitched twice, and it moved no more. Miss Bea let out a shrill, while the rhino gave it a prod with his horn.

'Well, if anyone's 'ungry!' he declared.

'Oh, no, no, thank you,' said Bea, turning away.

'Crikey, you can't eat that!' said Marcel.

'I would if I weren't a vegetarian; you won't get any fresher!' said Rhino.

'Anyway, we'd better get a move on. If he found us, the others might, too,' said the boy.

'This way then,' said Brim leading the way.

'Come on, Marcel, dear. We'll see you through the wall of darkness,' beckoned Bea, and Marcel soon found himself advancing cautiously into the deep dark tunnel, walking his fingers on the cold clayey wall for extra assurance.

Brimstone measured the step up front, followed by Bea, with Rhino plodding along behind Marcel. The boy held his penknife in his free hand in such a way as to project a slice of faint light from behind onto the path ahead. The dash of light it deflected was enough for him to situate the dark figures of his companions. It also helped him ward off the haunting thoughts of death and burial that had plagued his nights ever since he saw his father's coffin slide into the dark hole of the furnace. He steered his mind to concentrate solely on each step ahead, one after the other.

After thirty or so paces, he stopped and glanced back at the ground covered so far. He was buried in the thick darkness, could hardly make out his bristly hand before his eyes. It took him considerable effort to keep the panic attack from welling in his mind. Then something touched him. It nudged him gently again from behind. 'Keep going, Marcel. I think we're nearly there,' said the warm deep voice of the rhinoceros beetle. But what if the roof caved in now, what if there lay hideous creatures in wait ahead?

But no, he must not let fear take charge of his thoughts. He must keep them firmly fixed on his way ahead. And one step after the other, he was pushing back his fear of the dark, his fear of death, and ultimately his fear of the unknown.

'The outside air's getting stwonger, Marcel,' called Brim from up ahead.

'All right, you don't need to holler; you're bringing down lumps of earth with the echo,' Marcel said reproachfully in a loud whisper.

Noting the renewed firmness in the boy's voice, Bea said, 'There, we've nearly got you through your jitters.'

Indeed, Marcel found he now no longer needed to walk his fingers on the wall for balance. And the knotty wooliness of his belly was beginning to unravel into a firmer sort of mesh. Then some paces further on came a thump up ahead followed by, 'Ow!'

'What's up?'

'Just bumped me head!' hushed the inchworm with enthusiasm in spite of the bump. 'Guess what on?'

'What?'

'The end of the tunnel! I can smell the fwesh air on the other side all wight; we'll just have to dig thwough the wall!'

'It seems ever so thick, though. It'll take ages to get through!' said Bea.

'It probably will if you just stand there babbling at it!' said the rhino.

Meanwhile Marcel again glanced back at the ground they had covered. There he was, deep in the clutches of his childhood dread. The dash of light that had reassured him now had hardly the force to touch the ground. Yet no longer did the darkness suffocate him or cloak his senses in fear. Instead he breathed it in and, thanks to his antennae, found that he, too, sensed fresh air at the back of the tunnel, which left his chest swelling with new confidence. Until, that is, crumbs of earth began to fall from the ceiling above, followed by lumps. And Marcel suddenly felt a slimy snaky thing dangle before his very nose, flop onto his shoulder, and slither down his body.

'Argh!' he cried.

'Argh!' cried the thing, while Rhino turned and rammed it, but he bounced off again. 'Ouch, watch it, mate!' the thing cried.

'That's a worm!' said Brim.

'A worm with teeth!' added the worm, putting on a big albeit fluty voice. 'And biggens 'n' all, so I'd keep back if I was you.'

'Hah, never seen a worm with teeth!' said the inchworm.

'Relax, Worm, we've no intention of eating you!' said Rhino.

'Especially when you consider what they eat,' said Bea.

'Dead leaves,' said Brim. 'Yuk!'

'They ain't dead, just fallen, and someone's got to churn 'em over, else how would your flowers grow, eh, eh?' said the worm, spitting out a bit of grit. 'And what you fellas doin' down 'ere then anyway?'

'Showing the marcel around,' said the rhino warily.

'I'm his official guide,' piped in the inchworm.

'There ain't much to see down here, and you've hardly chosen the best spot either. Ground here's rock hard; it'd take a whole army of worms fifty seasons to churn it over and bore out enough irrigation galleries to turn it into something decently fertile,' said the worm, and he spat out another mouthful of soil. 'Gives me indigestion, it does, gritty on ya gizzard, it is. I'll be glad when I come to somink sweeter, I can tell ya.'

'You might have fallen in the right place then,' said the voice of Marcel in the darkness.

'Cor blimey, I didn't know marcels could speak common insect talk!'

'Er, I'd say it was you who was speaking marcel talk, more like,' said Marcel.

'No,' said the others in unison.

'Oh. Well. Never mind. What counts is that we can communicate. Now, where was I?' resumed Marcel, preferring not to dwell on that part of his 'insectification' he had so far overlooked.

'I might 'ave fallen in the right place,' said the worm expectantly and again spat out some gritty earth.

'Do worms like pollen extract?'

'Dunno, it don't grow down here. But a mate of mine came across some once up top and told me it was really yummy.'

'You should have asked 'im for some to twy.'

'I was going to, but the next minute he was in a tug o' war between a couple of black birds! Gives ya the jitters, don't it?'

'Bea, give our friend some pollen, would you?'

'Would if I could but we're on our last rations, Marcel.'

'Oh. Well, give him some of mine then.'

Bea did as was asked. Judging by the delectable slurping sounds and interjections of gratification, the worm was not far from discovering a new passion for mashed propolis.

'Oh, thank you, thank you, this is really...so incredibly yummy! Oh, so smooth, so soft and sweet—anymore where that came from?' he said, making a flapping noise with the flap of skin that covered his mouth, designed to keep it from getting bunged up when drilling.

'Well, as Miss Bea said, we're pretty much down to our last rations. But there again, if we got through to the light on the other side of the wall soon enough, we wouldn't be needing them. I'll tell you what, bore us a hole through the wall here to the fresh air on the other side, and I'll let you have some more of my rations.'

The worm naturally agreed but only after another helping of pollen extract. 'I could do with the extra booster, see. There's a lot more sub than topsoil to get through, you know,' he argued. Marcel consented, although in reality Bea only let go of another piece of propolis, normally used as a sealer for the nest. She kept back the more valued pollen for the finer palate. Because with such a simple mouthpiece usually filled with cruder matter, the bee deemed the worm most likely couldn't tell the difference between nectar and honey, let alone pollen and propolis.

'Yummy yum yum, pollen, gummy gum gum,' sang the worm, lovingly slavering over the propolis. He

then set to work squeezing together his anterior segments first then letting the posterior follow through
in an accordion fashion. In it went, into the earth wall
whose thickness represented the distance between con-
finement and liberty for the companions. And pretty
soon, first a hairbreadth, then a full halo of light filtered
in around the worm's body. And when the worm slipped
out the other side, a gleaming porthole replaced the dark
silhouette, only to be eclipsed again as the worm came
back in through the hole to reclaim his reward.

'There you go!' he said in his fluty voice as he
slithered his body back into the tunnel where the others
were waiting. Again light streamed in through the hole,
which Marcel found soon grew paler as his eyes recovered their faculty of gauging the influx. Nevertheless,
now with wide eyes, Marcel was able to see the slimy
worm square on, as with slippery fore segments, the
invertebrate lovingly petted the propolis laid down by
Miss Bea to moisten it. 'Yum, yummy yum yum, pollen, gummy...' he chanted, writhing his body in time
and then supped up the propolis purée noisily.

'Steady on; you'll give yourself a gooey gizzard,'
warned Miss Bea.

'He's done a fair enough job but not very wide,
though, is it?' said the rhinoceros after close inspection
of the wormhole. 'I'd be surprised if Miss Bea could get
her head through, let alone her rear end!'

'I beg your pardon!' said Bea indignantly.

'All right, calm down everyone. We've been in here a long time, but bear up just a little more; we're nearly out,' said Marcel.

'We would be if we had a proper opening to go through instead of a piddly little hole!' said the rhinoceros.

Having lapped up the best part of the propolis, the worm now looked up with a gormless grin. 'You want it wider? Gimme more of this pollen stuff and your wish is my command!'

The required width, which was translated into a number of holes, was agreed upon. The price was convened, and the worm bunched up his segments as before. Again he bored his way into the earth, this time a little to the left of the first perforation. The company, meantime, clustered around the wormhole and gave a contained cheer with every new breakthrough. Soon the aperture tripled, so letting in as much more fresh air from outside.

'I can smell fresh grass,' said Marcel, twitching his feelers.

'I can smell thistle leaves,' said Brimstone.

'I can smell a zest of lilac,' said Miss Bea.

'I can smell a snake!' said Rhino, putting a damper on their little guessing game.

'Do you always have to be so glum?' said the bee.

'Me, glum? I don't know what you're yapping on about, dame. And I can smell a snake, I tell you!'

'And so can we all,' said the inchworm. 'After all, we *are* in a snake tunnel. Look on the bwight side, though; we're nearly out!'

'Yes, nearly, but not quite,' said the rhino. 'Huh, glum, me?'

'Here, take the last rations before the worm gets back, to keep our minds on cheerier thoughts,' said Bea and discreetly offered round the last rations of pollen while the worm was busy boring the final lengths of the last hole.

'Thanks, Bea, but I've used up my rations,' said Marcel, despite a sharp pang of hunger.

'Correction, your rations of propolis but not of pollen!' she said, and so Marcel popped a sweet granule into his mouth, while Bea again lifted her head into the stream of warm air. 'Do you know, it's so nice to take in the scents of daytime again. I never realized before how precious they were.'

'Would you believe wight now I'd give up this dwop of pollen for just one nibble at a juicy blackthorn leaf?' said the inchworm.

'Just shows, it's not so easy to drive out your true nature, is it?' said the rhino.

'Are you suggesting I'm false?' said Brimstone.

'Oh, not false, Brim,' said Marcel, 'just in search of yourself, hmm?'

'Well, twue, and in that case, 'til I've found the twue me, who do you think I am now? Yummy yum yum, pollen, gummy gum,' sang the inchworm, comically writhing his body just like the worm, which put the smile back on everyone's faces.

The company gathered around the worm as he made his way back through the last perforation. They cheered his precision performance of lacing back and forth through the inch-thick wall to the adjoining tunnel to produce five holes with a wafer thin partition of earth between each. It just took a push and they fell through, leaving an aperture wide enough for even the rhino to squeeze through.

'Here's your due,' said the bee, laying down the prize of a scoop of propolis.

'Do you know,' said the worm, moistening the propolis as per his new ritual. 'Do you know, I used to get the jitters once, and I'd 'a' never 'ave gone through that wall, even for all the pollen extract Miss Bea could hold in her stockings,' he continued between slurps, becoming slightly tipsy. 'Just goes to show you, it's worth getting on top of 'em, the jitters I mean, coz when you do, there's all sorts of things what lies in store.

'Scared of snakes I was, until the day I came face-to-face with one in a snake tunnel just like this one. But luckily for me, I'd been enjoying some henbane leaf, which makes you forget your worries. I reckon that's what kept me from freezing from fright. Anyway, I just managed to slip meself into a hollow just deeper than the length of its tongue. But as it went scuffing past, the sides of my little refuge crumbled clean away and left me like a sitting duck. Course, the snake sensed I was in the open. Thought I was dead meat, I did. I sensed it hissing its tongue around and getting really wound up, because try as it would, there was no way it could slide backward because of its scales that kept catching. And there was no room for it to turn around in neither. Well, in the end, I sat there having a real good laugh, as it could do naught else but continue on its way. And believe it or not, I looks out for 'em now, snakes, I do,' concluded the worm, quite pleased with himself.

'I thought worms couldn't see!' said Marcel.

'Oh, yes we can!'

'But you've got no eyes to see with.'

'And I don't particularly want none neither; they'd be forever getting clogged up. No, I've got sensors under me skin, else how would I know if I was upstairs or down?' said the worm. 'Hah, and I can even tell ya that first snake was the spitting image of the one that's lying in wait at the entrance.'

On hearing this, the whole company scrambled—except for the rhino, who waded—through the aperture, which led into an adjoining tunnel that ran left into total darkness. They all looked right along the incoming path that sloped round slightly and upward into broad daylight to take stock of their dilemma: a snake indeed was lying with its scaly head at the entrance out there.

'Come on, fellas, let's have a bit of a laugh, watch this!' slurred the worm, half sozzled on propolis. And after sliding out from the wall into the adjoining gallery, he began a wormy dance to tease the snake, knowing full well he had a hole to slither into just in case the reptile struck. 'Ooh, ooh, sleepy head,' called the worm in his fluty singsong fashion, but the snake was apparently dozing.

'Worm, I warn you, you're tempting the devil,' said Marcel in a low voice with an eye on the massive reptile.

'What's the matter, not scared of a little biddy grass snake are ya? Come on fellas,' said the worm, 'you're all right with me. I've been closer than this, huh. Besides, she's asleep!'

'It's true,' said Rhino. 'Look carefully and you'll see the see-through scale over each eye.'

'Now watch this,' said the worm, who wriggled his body to the middle of the tunnel floor, fully exposing himself to the dozing snake. He then went into a wormish dance, going round in circles. Suddenly, there came a crumbling of earth from the dark end of the gallery, accompanied by a rapid patter of feet.

Marcel flashed his eyes into the darkness in time to make out a great hairy monster come hurtling out. And with astonishing spring in his legs, he bounded headfirst in through the wormholes, close behind Brim, while the heedless worm was snapped up by the tail.

9

The Snake and the Vole

The company sat petrified behind the partition as the patter of feet died away. A long silence fell with the settling dust.

'I wonder if the worm's still wriggling inside,' said Bea at last with a shudder.

'I once heard a bird say that's what they like best about worms, the tickle inside their bellies!' said Brim.

'Just goes to show,' said Rhino in his deep voice of reason, 'you might get over your jitters, but you still gotta respect 'em, and respect 'em like a faithful companion whose word of warning might one day save your chitin!'

Turning to Marcel, Bea remarked, 'And I say, how you hopped it, Marcel.'

'Yeah, never seen you shift it like that before,' said the inchworm.

After a moment Marcel turned from the darkness. 'It's my legs,' he said gravely. 'It's like they were ten times stronger,' he continued, caught between the anguish of his ongoing metamorphosis and the thrill of the new power that had just saved his skin.

'I think we'd better be making a move to the woyal jelly then,' said the inchworm, not forgetting his own metamorphosis and the promise of a share of the noble nectar.

'But how are we supposed to get out now with the vole at one end and the snake at the other?' asked Bea.

'I personally detest voles,' said the rhinoceros.

'Oh, I've heard that voles are vewy fond of whinos though,' quipped Brim.

'Remember what the worm said,' said Marcel, again turning his gaze from the darkness. 'If we can lure the snake into the tunnel and its head past us, then we're safe. It can't turn around; it'll have to keep going to another outlet somewhere further up.'

'But how can we get the snake in,' asked the bee.

'By using the vole as live bait,' said Marcel.

'But the vole ain't daft enough to come lumberin' up the tunnel where the snake can see it,' said Rhino.

'It might if it's lured by something tasty,' said Marcel. 'What do voles eat?'

'Worms, apparently,' said the rhinoceros, and all eyes spontaneously turned on Brimstone, who was munching on some bitter root.

'Hold it fellas; I'm not a worm. I mean, do I look like a worm?'

'You do a very good impersonation of one,' said Bea.

'Oh, not weally. I'm too short, see?' said Brim, squeezing his head into his body to make himself even shorter.

'I personally think you'd make a fine worm,' seconded Rhino.

'Don't worry, Brimstone, you'll only be *acting* as live bait. I mean you won't be *it* for real. Listen, here's the plan: while you're attracting the vole, I'll be doing the same with the snake. But as soon as the snake sees the vole, you can bet where it'll have its sights fixed. The vole, before it gets anywhere near you, will make a run for it the other way, leading the snake with it, so leaving the coast clear for us to leg it out of here,' said Marcel, who clapped his hands and sprung onto his feet, ready for action.

'Er, Marcel, I'm not sure I can handle this. See, the pwoblem is, I may be able to take off a worm, but I definitely can't hop it like a cwicket!'

'Brimstone, as my irrevocable guide, which way is out?'

'That way,' admitted the inchworm, miserably pointing toward the broad daylight.

'As my irrevocable guide, you ought to be leading me, right?'

'All wight, all wight. But I'm no good for anything at the moment; I'm famished. If I don't have something, I shall go off.'

'You can have a scratch round in my baskets,' said the bee, and not without some reticence, she let the inchworm enjoy the last crumbs of pollen.

'Let's just hope it won't be wasted like on the worm!' said Rhino in a glum afterthought.

***

Marcel was once again scrambling from the relative safety of the dark and disused snake tunnel into the relative precariousness of the half-lit adjoining gallery. He shot across to the darker side and stole up forty or so paces to where a chunk of earth must have fallen away, leaving a recess in the wall. Into this space, he wedged his body out of the reptile's sights.

The inchworm slipped out of the aperture in turn and edged his way cautiously a few lengths in the opposite direction toward the thickening obscurity. There he stood with one eye on the gloom and the other on the aperture made by the worm, ready to shift it. Further up the gallery, Marcel motioned to the bee, who was peering through the aperture, to get her to prompt Brimstone into action.

'Don't just stand there, wriggle about like a worm!' she called. The inchworm attempted a jig, but still nothing stirred. Growing in confidence, he inched another few strides into the darkness.

'I think it's gone!' he called back a few moments later. But barely had his belly quelled at the reassuring thought than a distant scamper came travelling swiftly up the corridor.

'Now, run Brim!' called the boy. He sprang from his post full into the light, hollering and waving his arms where the grass snake, only thirty paces in front of him, could not fail to see him. Provided, that is, it was awake. Meanwhile the inchworm was but three looping strides from the aperture with the scampering of feet

echoing louder and louder. But the panic-stricken creature stepped on his own front prolegs and tripped.

'Hurry, Brimstone. The vole's closing in!' bellowed
Rhino, while Bea flipped out from her safe viewpoint.
She went into a spin around the inchworm in the hope
of winning him precious seconds to pick himself up before the beady-eyed monster was upon him.

'Vole!' bawled Rhino, as the hairy monster suddenly pounced out from the darkness. But it quickly
checked its step on seeing the bee, whose sting could be
extremely painful. Brim had by now recovered his stride
and was but two lengths from the aperture as the rodent
rounded the winging bee and hunched up its back for
a strike.

Marcel had moved dangerously within striking
distance of the snake. He was trying desperately to alert
the creature with cries and gesticulation and lumps of
earth. Then, as he quickly glanced back at the bee giving cover to the inchworm at the peril of her own life,
there came a sudden movement from the entrance. He
turned in time to see the snake flare up its eyes, flicker
its tongue. Then with spectacular rapidity, it jerked its
great head forward. Marcel bounded for the recess, where
he flattened his body against the wall and turned to see
but a blur of green and yellow as the striking reptile
whooshed past him and hurtled on down the gallery.

'Snake! Get against the wall!' came the bellowing
voice of Rhino again. The vole on the pounce literally
changed direction in midair, its expression from malice

to terror, and went scuttling back down the gallery before the double-hinged jaws of its predator.

Marcel, stepping out from his recess, looked on at
the scene over near the aperture, expecting the worst.
The dust began to settle. As he hurried back, his eyes
picked out a dark inert form lying against the wall
where the snake had shuttled by. Then, from the aperture, the single horn of the rhino showed followed by
the inchworm, and they all three gathered round the
dusty mass.

'Miss Bea, poor Miss Bea,' said Rhino dolefully.

'She saved my life,' sniffed Brimstone.

'A brave act, that,' said Marcel, who never once
imagined he would one day find himself grieving for a
honeybee. 'We shall miss her,' he said, bowing his head.

'For all her clumsiness, I shall miss her noble
heart,' the rhinoceros solemnly declared.

But then the lone mass began to move. 'Would
you mind saying that again?' it returned in an imperi-
ous voice.

'Miss Bea, you're alive!' rejoiced the inchworm.

'Pwah, good on ya, dame!' said the rhino.

It was indeed a dusty bee if ever there was that
swiveled her head, flipped her wings, and rose onto her
feet.

'Good on you, Bea!' cheered Marcel, brushing
away a few crumbs of earth that had got lodged in her
wing sockets. 'Now let's get out of here before the snake
makes a round trip for its afters!'

10

A Dangerous Leap

The four companions pushed on up the gallery. At last they met with the warmth of sun that kindled their spirits, the light of day that fed their eyes, and the scents of summer made stronger by the passage of the ox-drawn mower and scythe. The area being of rough parkland, the machine's blades had been set high so that the grass would not turn to straw. While Rhino was trying to unjam his wing casings, Marcel clambered to the top of a tuft to get a good view of the surrounding area. He was agreeably surprised to discover that their subterranean adventure had brought them just twenty meters or so from the square of lawn on the west flank of Villeneuve where after-lunch coffee was often served. It was surrounded by box hedging. The evaporating moisture being sapped from the earth by the summer sun gave a fuzzy blur to the scene. The view of the house clad in foliage behind the cedar tree resembled one of those paintings by Monsieur Monet, thought Marcel. He then turned his head and perceived a young girl in white strolling along the alley of horse chestnut trees holding a hat. His hat.

'Marcel, Marcel,' he heard her call out before the stem of coarse grass he was leaning on bowed under his weight and delivered him to the ground.

'I wouldn't expose myself like that if I was you, Marcel,' said the inchworm with a dubious glance at the sky.

But overjoyed at the sight of Julia, Marcel leapt into the air in a giant bound to get another glimpse. However, Julia was no longer there and, having misjudged the strength of his legs, he came tumbling back down in a heap on the floor.

'You weally shouldn't hop like that,' said Brim.

'At least not until you've learnt how to land!' added Rhino.

'Wow, didn't think I'd get so high,' said Marcel, picking himself up. 'I was, er, just getting our bearings.'

'I've alweady got 'em,' said Brim.

'So have I,' said Bea, glad to recover her sense of direction from the sun.

'We'd better be making twacks for cover,' said Brimstone, chewing on a mouthful of grass blade. 'We can thwead our way between the tufts along there.'

'Between the tufts? That'll virtually double the distance!' Marcel said.

'Wouldn't it be better to cut straight across that patch where the grass is scanty? Look, one can see right through to the finer grass of the lawn on the other side of the box hedging,' said Bea.

'Nope. Shorter perwaps. Better, certainly not. See, you're not used to life on the ground as I am, Miss Bea,' said the inchworm and then enigmatically added, 'Birds!' He insisted that no matter who they passed, whatever flowers lay strewn along the way, they must not stop. They must keep moving in his step until they cleared the meadow.

'But—'

'No buts, wemember who's the iwwevocable guide!'

And so it was without further questions that the bee, the rhino, and the marcel filed along behind the inchworm. As fast as their tired legs could carry them, they meandered between razed clusters of grass and decapitated flowers, despite the growing temptation to replenish their bellies. Marcel, for his part, delighted in the powerful scents his antennae clearly distinguished, and he never ceased to marvel at the weird and wonderful creatures they passed. Such as a pair of red gendarme bugs with their strange black tribal markings that advanced back-to-back madly in love. A dung beetle that was busy rolling a dollop of ox dung for digs for its offspring. And a grasshopper on a purple thistle flower who twitched its head to Marcel and said, 'Where are you lot off to in such a hurry? You ought to be enjoying the feast!'

'Er, we're off to get some royal jelly,' said the boy, who had slowed his step to admire the insect's tender green livery and muscular femur.

'Royal jelly? Don't know why you bother. Look around ya; there's pollen and nectar galore. You just have to bend down and scoop it up, pal,' chuckled the footloose and pleasure-grazing grasshopper. It proceeded in drawing the pegs of its hind legs over the toothed veins of its forewings. This produced a strident chirp and set its wings vibrating. Marcel watched on, thoroughly enthralled by the fiddler's hypnotic one-note music whose modulation intensified as the pegs played over the rasping veins.

'Come on, Marcel. Got to keep moving!' called the inchworm three tufts further ahead.

'Won't be a sec,' returned Marcel. Intrigued by the powerful sound produced by the grasshopper, he asked if it would play it again.

'All right, but only if you tell me what's all the fuss with this royal jelly!' said the beguiling grasshopper, coolly chewing some purple thistle petals.

'Oh, I...I have to eat some to grow,' said Marcel, who now gazed into the insect's bulbous eyes.

'What's a hopper wanna grow for. If you wanna be taller, why don't ya just hop?'

'Hopper? No, no, I'm not really a hopper—'

'But I saw you hop, pal,' said the grasshopper dubiously.

'Yes, but I'm not really as you see me now. I'm really a human.'

'A human? Very interesting, that. You don't often get to chat with a human. Well, here goes for the music lover then!' said the grasshopper, who apparently needed little coaxing when it came to exhibiting his musical talents. 'This one's called Alf's little note!'

'Maarcel!' yelled the inchworm up ahead.

'Maaarcel!' shrilled the bee.

Marcel no longer heard them. Alf the grasshopper had begun his little 'note'. To the unknowing ear, it consisted of a loud modulation of the wing that grew to soul-stirring heights. Alf stopped in mid-crescendo, leaving Marcel with a longing for more.

'All right, you tell me where you're heading, and I'll continue my little note,' said the grasshopper, staring into Marcel's eyes. But as Marcel was about to tell, a looming shadow gave the insect some cause for alarm. It suddenly sprang off its perch. The boy gazed up at the fabulous leap and found himself thinking how excellent it must be to have wings. But the very next instant, a swooping swallow snapped up the grasshopper in mid-flight. It was tossed and crushed then gobbled up! Not surprisingly this immediately shook Marcel out of his blissful trance.

'Oh, crikey!' he said and legged off to catch up with his companions. Having witnessed the grasshopper's last hop, too, they were already weaving as fast as they could between the protective tufts of the prairie where elated swallows were feasting over the freshly cut grass.

'Now I see why we've taken the long tufty route!' said Marcel, running and panting behind them.

'Keep doggo and huwwy before they start dipping!' hollered the inchworm up ahead just as another shadow drew over them. This was immediately followed by the ear-cracking snap of a beak barely an inch above Marcel's antennae.

Keeping a low profile, the company meandered and dashed from tuft to tuft until at last they stood on safe ground in the midst of the shaded refuge of box hedging.

11
Crossing the Desert

'Wow, that was close. I say, you're lucky you're still in one piece, Marcel,' said Bea.

'You mean that bird,' said Marcel.

'No, she meant the gwasshopper,' said Brim. 'Never talk to gwasshoppers, let alone look into their eyes.'

'Or else they'll hypnotize ya and rip ya belly out before you can blink,' said Rhino. 'The worst is at night. That's when they prowl, see. Their favorite is cicada, cause cicadas suck sap all day long, so by the time night comes, it's well soaked into their bellies.'

'But it had such a beautiful song,' said Marcel.

'That weren't no song; it was a note,' said Rhino. 'I managed to decipher some of it. It mentioned who you are and what you're looking for. Don't know what for, but there can't be any good in it.'

They were standing under the cover of an age-old row of neatly cropped box that offered them a clear way of bare though bumpy earth along two meters either side.

To their right, only the thick fair trunks posted down the middle impeded a perfectly clear view all the way to the smooth and compact dirt path that ran along the west flank of the house. But with nothing but box leaves to feed on, they decided to continue crosswise under the hedging.

Some minutes later found them contemplating a lush expanse of flat-topped turf glistening in hues of green and gold. It contrasted deliciously with the flaxen prairie they had left behind. A light fragrance perfumed the air, that of roses planted between the turf and the hedge. To Bea's regret, the thorny stems, however, forbade a climb to visit the exquisite rose nectarines. Needless to say, the inchworm wasn't too put out, though.

'Lush gween gwass. That'll do me,' he said, licking his lips.

'And the going looks nice and flat, too,' observed Marcel.

'Hmmm,' said Rhino, 'I wouldn't build your hopes up too much.'

'Oh, come on, gwumps!' cheered Brimstone, who felt a whole lot better at the sight of the endless supply of pasture. And despite the rhino's warning, the inchworm led the way to the edge of the turf. Marcel waded into the tender lush blades up to his waist. But hardly had he taken a dozen strides into the soft sea of green than he was made to halt.

'Beugh...pwah, this is disgusting!' cried Brim, who had stopped for a bite.

'And it smells positively awful!' said Bea.

'I tried to warn yous!' called out an amused rhino, which was suspiciously out of character.

But it was the next event that tipped the balance in favor of a dash back under the cover of the hedge. There came a clipping sound and a sharp human voice. 'Ouch, bother!' it yelped. Marcel turned his head to find towering not two meters from where he was standing, none other than Madame Deforge under a straw hat. With pruning shears in hand, she was about to bend down in his direction to retrieve the rose she had just dropped.

'Quick, back under cover everyone!' called Marcel, bounding back to where the rhino hadn't budged a foot.

'What is that?' said Brim, looking out cautiously from under the box hedge.

'Huh, can't you see, it's a marcelette!' said Miss Bea.

'It's Henriette's mother,' said Marcel. 'Henriette is the girl whose party I'm going to, by the way.'

'Don't blame you for running away,' said Rhino.

'I ran away because if she sees me like this she'll either have a stroke or stamp on me. Don't take it personally, but she hates bugs! Besides that, Bea's right, it stinks out there!'

'And it tastes wevolting!'

'That's because they put cow pee in with the water! I've seen 'em do it, I have!' chuckled Rhino, which sent the inchworm into another bout of spitting.

'Peuh, pwah...pwah...I've gotta get wid of this taste. And I'm famished. I could eat a cabbage all to meself! And all we got is boggin' box leaves; they'we indigestible!' said Brim.

'Well you're the one who brought us here!' said Miss Bea.

'You've got a cheek, and who got us into this pickle in the first place?' said the inchworm. But before a dispute fully broke out, there came another cry from high above that silenced their squabble. Then another flower head meant for the basket rolled under the hedge in front of them. Marcel did not waste a second.

'Don't just stand there, give me a hand!' he yelled, motioning toward the magnificent mature flower. The creatures took hold and heave-hoed their prize an extra two inches to safety under the box hedge to feast on while above a conversation ensued.

'Ah, Julia. You gave me quite a fright.'

'Sorry, Aunt Delphine, I was looking for Marcel.'

'Marcel? My dear girl, it seems to be coming quite a habit of yours.'

'Oh, I don't think so. It's that he's wanted by Uncle to settle some problem with his new cutting machine.'

'Have you tried the barn?'

'Yes.'

'Of course you have, dear. What about the oak tree? He often stalks around there.'

'Yes, that's where I found his hat, but he seems to have disappeared.'

'Nonsense, child, he's probably popped home without it. You know how distracted he can be. Just because his mother asked us to keep an eye on him doesn't oblige him to stay posted on the premises.'

'I've just been over; I'm sure he hasn't gone home.'

'Then he is indoors. Just let me finish beheading these withered roses and we'll have a look together. He can't be far.'

Marcel meanwhile had pulled himself out of the flower where his companions were getting their fill of matured nectar and pollen. He was now sitting on a silky rose petal, letting the voice of Julia flutter into his ears. Whilst trying to remind himself that he was the level-headed mathematical type able to dominate his emotions, he peeped through the trellis of box leaves just making out the dark-robed outline of Madame Deforge and the white toilette of Julia before they moved on to another rose bush. Keeping under the hedge, he trailed them in the hope of getting a glimpse of Julia. But as soon as he had caught them up and managed to focus his sight on her pretty head, they were off again. And again he was bounding over the bumpy earth toward the house as noiselessly as he could, so as not to lose the thread of their conversation.

'Oh it *is* hot this afternoon. One might have thought that the heat would have abated by now.'

'Malzac says it is the hottest day of the year so far.'

'And how is my sister, by the way?'

'Mother has her good days, but she's still weak.'

'My dear, I am so glad we could come to her aid, but I can imagine it must be so bitter for her to have to take the little farmhouse since your father passed away without a kopeck to his name.'

Madame Deforge snipped off another rose, which dropped into her basket, and then moved on to the next tree, leaving Marcel to scuttle his way beneath the hedging to keep up.

'You know, Julia, I think you quite like young Marcel, don't you?'

'Well, yes, my aunt, why shouldn't I? He has been very helpful with all kinds of repairs since we moved in. He's really very ingenious—'

'Yes, child, but he is poor!'

'I don't understand.'

'Oh, I think you do. Need I remind you how much your poor mother has had a run of bad luck? Well, so has Marcel. Now, I think he deserves a change in fortune, don't you? And his taking to our way of life will help him greatly; don't you think so? You never know, I may one day have the satisfaction of him calling me mother.'

'Yes, Aunt Delphine, and I wish my dear cousin all the happiness in the world if that is what Marcel wants,' answered Julia with a dry smile.

'Good, my dear, just you bear that in mind. Now, let us find the young man before your uncle gets into one of his flusters.'

By now an extenuated Marcel was at the edge of the hedging, which terminated at a wrought-iron flowerpot in the shape of an elephant's foot. He looked across the dusty dirt path just in time to see the two gargantuan figures, one barrel-hipped and the other slender, glide up the stone steps surrounded by bulging iris plants and in through some French windows to the drawing room.

The pearl-grey metal shutters were pulled loosely together to keep out the intense heat of the day. From the shade of the flowerpot, Marcel glanced back at the feast going on without him some two hundred or so paces further back, which in real terms equaled barely two meters. Bea, Rhino, and Brimstone were diligently tucking into the nectar, oblivious to his departure.

Madame Deforge's words had stoked his sense of independence while making it clear to him where she intended to lead him in the end: up the aisle with Henriette! Surely Julia wouldn't be taken in, too. He had to know. He turned his eyes back to the scorching sterile expanse of bare path that formed a perilous crossing, testified by the odd worm lying frazzled here and there. However, the sun was past its zenith and, yielding to his indignation while quite forgetting his present predicament, he stepped out from the shade of the elephant foot to embark on a trek across the 'desert'.

But the stark sunshine immediately pounded his head and shoulders as he went on his way, briskly at first, until the going got too heavy for him to walk, let alone march. He had underestimated the immense power of the sun on his reduced person, and soon he could feel his life fluids being drawn out of him.

On looking back, he saw he had covered two-thirds of the way but realized, too, that the remaining third would cost him double the effort. He had definitely made a mistake, one that could leave him as frizzled as one of those frazzled worms. This could be his last battle, but he decided he would not go down without a fight.

As he had done in the dark tunnel before, he fixed his thoughts on one goal—survival—and gritting his teeth, he staggered forward, counting each step in the knowledge that there could not be one hundred in all to reach the other side to the luxuriant undergrowth. If only he had taken some refreshment at the rose. He tried to ward off such negative thoughts, but despite his efforts of concentration, his mind wandered, his sight became blurred, and he suddenly wondered if he was going the right way at all.

'Marcel, Marcel,' he heard the sharp voice of Madame Deforge call from ahead, no doubt from inside the house, but could he trust it? In his delirium, he wondered if she was deliberately leading him from his path. Hadn't she tried to map out his life for him? Even his own father would never have tried to impose his own plan on him. In a haze of memories, Marcel recalled how his dad had introduced him to sport, natural history, mechanics, music, even literature, to encourage him to find out where his talents lay so that he could cultivate them, build up a noble passion, which meant sticking at it, even if the road ahead sometimes seemed a lonely and tough one to take. *He who betrays not himself, will find fidelity in others along the way*, Marcel recalled him saying.

'Probably never thought I'd end up stuck in the middle of a flaming desert,' the boy said to himself disconsolately. But then the thought of Madame Deforge trying to puppeteer his future refueled his defiance. Regaining control of his senses, he continued the staggering march forward, putting his thoughts away to reserve all his energy for his feet that plodded resolutely on. Until…

'Marcel, Marcel,' intoned a deep voice coming up against his flank, and the massive frame of Rhino lumbered into the tail of his eye. 'Climb aboard, Marcel. We're nearly there!' Without a word, the boy literally collapsed astride the beetle's broad back, and in this way he was delivered to the tall thick shade of the iris plants below the drawing room windows.

***

'Thanks, Rhino, the heat out there, it really gave me a clobbering,' said one mighty fatigued marcel, hammocked in an iris leaf.

'The heat and lack of nutrition!' said Bea with an admonishing look and handed him another rose pollen drop from the stack in her stocking.

'And I thought humans could live on fwesh air for ages. Hah, I say, Marcel, looks like you weally are turning into one of us!' said Brimstone. 'I'd have thought though with your bwains you'd have made yourself a sunshade, I did!' continued Brimstone and proudly explained how he had used a box tree leaf stuck onto his back with propolis in order to follow Miss Bea and Rhino, who were used to the sun, to Marcel's rescue. Marcel congratulated him on his presence of mind and owned that he himself had quite lost his head, had underestimated the heat and the distance.

'You see, I saw Julia under the influence of Madame Deforge. I wanted to follow her to warn her not to listen.'

'There, relax a little more until you've recovered all your strength, Marcel,' mothered Miss Bea. She was dabbing his roasting forehead in a soothing gelatinous liquid she had obtained by stroking a pearl of it on a leaf.

'And before you go warning any marcelette, you got some growing up to do, remember?' said Rhino. 'Or else you might get walked on!'

'Too much sun, it's made 'im soft in the head,' said Miss Bea.

'But we said we'd get you to the woyal jelly, and we will, won't we fellas?'

Listening to his new friends comforted him in his fatigue, and with the sun still broiling his brain, he let his head fall back and be dabbed.

'Anyway, thanks for coming, all of you. Now I understand what someone very dear once told me about finding fidelity.'

As he said this, a drop of the liquid trickled over his brow. He instinctively wiped it with a finger, which he put to the tip of his tongue. Then sitting bolt upright, he cried out, 'That's water!' and leaned forward on his knees, plunging his burning head into the cool bubble on a leaf beside the bee. The refreshing effect was instantaneous but so too was his discovery of the suction power of water. The bubble engulfed his head to his shoulders and, for some desperate seconds, would not for the life of him let him have it back. He managed to keep his hands clear, but with nothing to grip on to, he found his head suspended inside the bubble until Bea reached out a claw for him to grab onto, and he yanked himself out.

'You mustn't rush at water!' said the bee, while Marcel rubbed it all over his face and head.

'Aye, else it'll suck you in and clog up your air holes!' said the rhino.

'I saw a mosquito get its leg caught in a blob once. Nearly pulled it out of its socket twying to yank it fwee,' said the inchworm. 'Then it got its other legs stuck 'til only its head was in the dwy!'

'At least it could breathe,' remarked Marcel, tugging at an earlobe.

'Bweathe? No, it dwowned actually, got all clogged up.'

'Oh, silly me, yes, I forget your breathing system differs,' returned Marcel, remembering insects have air holes, otherwise known as spiracles, along the sides of their bodies for them to take in oxygen.

'How do marcels bweathe then?' said Brim with a fleeting look along the side of Marcel's fully clad thorax.

'Through the nose and mouth.'

'That must be twicky. The mouth is for eating, not bweathing.'

'Didn't you know that?' said Miss Bea. 'That's why he pants and snorts when he gets worked up. Marcels lack air holes, you know.'

'Yes, and I nearly just drowned in a bubble!' he said cheerfully now that he was feeling fresher thanks to the dunking. Moreover, the recently watered flowerbed offered a cooler climate, and Marcel was soon back on his feet, gazing up at the great west wall of Villeneuve beautifully clad in rose and ivy.

The first small upper window on the right belonged to the boxroom that led onto the guest room. The next three windows, equal in width and in height, presented the same symmetry as the drawing room openings below. From memory, there was the maid's room behind the first of them. The next window looked into the corridor that whisked right through the house some twenty-five meters to its counterpart.

Behind the furthest window was Henriette's room. Marcel had not been in there since he and she were caught playing prince and princess five years past. Marcel remembered the window offered a beautiful view across the orchards and Mon Plaisir field further to the rear of the house where Julia must have seen the sunflowers coming into bloom.

Henriette's window also featured the Largnac village church some three kilometers away, which poked its spire above the tree line. And in the winter months on a clear day, Deforge's brick works this side of the village could be spied through the leafless trees. Ironically, thought Marcel, the next time he was to admire that view, if Madame Deforge had her way, was to be as Henriette's prince for real. Sure, he could one day become master of the house and would indeed love it, as a faithful friend whose friendship lay rooted in childhood, precisely as he certainly did care for Henriette.

But Julia was right, though it could mean roughing it at first. To succeed, he must go on with his scholarship in the city. He must make his own tracks, and the sooner the better, he resolved with determination. His whole life's work depended on it. A rustle in the undergrowth somewhere behind interrupted his cogitation, his eyes fell back on his companions, and he thought nothing more of it.

The rhino and the inchworm were watching Miss Bea, who had climbed onto the side of a flowerpot and was performing a waggle dance.

'What's going on?' asked Marcel.

'We're working out how far it is to the nest,' said Rhino.

'But I know where the lime tree is. It's over there on the other side of the house.'

'If you don't mind me being blunt, "over there" isn't a very exact estimate, Marcel,' said Rhino.

'Shhh!' snapped Brim, who counted under his breath when the bee came round again for another run. Then the prima donna stopped.

'There,' she said, satisfied with herself.

'There what?' said Marcel.

'Shh, I'm twying to think,' hushed the inchworm. 'That makes woughly…er…one thousand five hundwed and forty-five stwides to the woyal jelly. That should be all wight. I've still got another two thousand odd stwides left in me before the changes start.'

'Aye, but don't forget that's in a straight line, which means travelling across the front of the house,' remarked Rhino.

'It's the shortest way,' said Miss Bea.

'That's all right if you can fly, but if you're on the ground, there's no cover,' said the rhino. 'The path is in the open and still blazing in the sun. We'd be prey for the picking. I say we go round the back of the house. There's plenty of cover there.'

'He's wight,' said Brim. 'Only, that's out of my wange. I'm never gonna make it to the woyal jelly!'

'Hang on; let's not panic. We've got to get across to the other side of the house where the lime tree is, right? But there *is* an even shorter way. We need neither go round the front nor round the back of the house, we'll go through it!' said Marcel to his companions, who returned a look of consternation. Marcel continued on a positive note. 'Look, it's flat and under cover all the way. There are no snakes, voles, or birds, and it will lead us to the other side in no time. And there's no baking sun, either. Hah, I'd say the only risk is the mop,' he chuckled, indulging in a little comic relief. But it did not quite have the desired effect.

'Mop? Never heard of a mop. What kind of cweature's that then?' asked the inchworm.

'Hah, you mean you don't know what a mop is?' said Miss Bea in a superior sort of voice.

'Nope. Go on; what is it then?'

'Why a mop is…a mop is…'

'An amphibious thing with long, thick hairs all over,' intervened Marcel so that Bea would not lose face and create a fuss.

'What's its mission in life?' asked Brim.

'Mission?'

'Yes, every creature has a mission,' insisted the bee now that the embarrassing question of the mop was out of her court.

'Well I suppose their mission is to gobble up rotten stains left over the floor.'

'Like a dung beetle then,' said the rhinoceros.

'In a way,' said Marcel and added for good measure, 'but there's no worry; they only come out once a day. And the one in the house lives under the stairs, and we won't be going anywhere near there.'

'Hmmm, well, besides mops, I've heard there's all sorts of traps and invisible walls that prevent you from escaping!' said the rhino on a dubious note.

'Invisible walls?'

'It's true, I've seen all sorts of insects trying to get out until they fall from exhaustion,' seconded Bea.

'Ah, you mean windows!' said Marcel cottoning on and revealed part of their mystery.

'Now, as long as we stick together, we'll be all right,' he continued, 'I know the house just as well as Bea knows her nest, and given that Brim wants to reach the royal jelly before he starts to metamorphose, I don't see we've got much choice.'

12

A House Full of Danger

The metal shutters were pulled ajar, letting a slit of daylight into the cool drawing room. From the mantelpiece, the familiar ping of the clock announced a quarter to the hour. The smells of lavender beeswax, Earl Grey tea, and linseed oil seemed for Marcel to convey a feeling of comfort and reassurance, though they were not met with quite the same enthusiasm by his insect friends.

'Pwah, I can't stand this boggin' stench any longer. Makes you feel sick!' said Rhino. They were travelling along the skirting toward the door leading into the hall.

'And I don't know how you manage to walk on two legs on this floor; I can hardly walk on six!' said Bea, paddling as best as she could behind.

'That's because it's just been waxed. Try and keep as close to the wall as you can. I've noticed they're not half as generous with the elbow grease there,' said Marcel.

The inchworm came to a sudden halt. 'Wow, look up there. That's a Purple Empewor,' he said, casting an admiring eye up at the specimen on the opposite wall. 'Ain't she a beauty!'

'Ahh!' cried Bea. 'Nobody move. A hornet—up there!' She pointed up at the mantle where a giant hornet with a black blank gaze presided on a pedestal.

'Gor bligh, *I* never sensed any danger, must be getting past it,' said Rhino.

'This time we're cooked!' whimpered Bea.

'Wun for cover; it hasn't seen us yet!'

'Hang on, everyone. Just stay where you are and look again.' They all looked up at the insects still holding their poses.

'They're not moving!'

'No, and you never sensed any danger, Rhino, because there isn't any. They're...um...they're dead,' said Marcel.

'Dead,' said Bea with a sigh of relief. 'Phew. I expect they couldn't get through the invisible walls.'

'And there's a stag!'

'And look at that rose chafer!'

Desperately changing the subject from the immortalized insects displayed around the room, Marcel said, 'Not far now and we're out into the hall. If I could land on my feet properly, I bet I could be there in three hops. But what's the point of being able to hop if you can't land properly?'

'That's because you need some wings, dear,' said Bea.

'Wings? Oh, you mean...crikey!' gulped Marcel, who instantly got the chilling vision of himself flying about hopelessly in search of pollen in the autumn, if as an insect he would live that long.

While he upped the pace and ruminated on the worrying possibility of sprouting wings, about the room the immaculate floorboards creaked and shuddered with the comings and goings of the maid preparing tea outside.

At Villeneuve, taking tea in the summer garden had been instated as an afternoon ritual not to be missed. A convenient rendezvous where Deforge could air his theories and political views while seated in his favorite wicker armchair with his most faithful, uncomplaining, complaisant audience sitting around him on the stone banks laid out on each side of the garden. They invariably consisted of resident and visiting family, cooperative friends, Father Brulin, the village mayor, and Marcel. Of late a new face had shown itself most willing and able, that of Wilfried Delpech. Despite his youth, Wilfried, a scout who was preparing to take the cloth, had mercifully stepped into the role of punctuator. This meant prodding the discourse along at a comfortable pace so as to give the speaker the feeling of completion while allowing the audience the opportunity of shutting down systems and just keeping their minds on maintaining their eyelids open.

Monsieur and Madame Deforge entered the room together from the hall.

'Is there anything wrong with Henriette?' said the stout, imposing figure of Philibert Deforge, closing the hallway door. 'She seems to have changed.'

'In what way, dear?' said his wife, fanning herself.

'I keep catching her smiling, quite unlike her.'

'I've noticed it, too. I've a feeling there's romance in the air; she's at that time of life. She'll be spreading her wings sooner than you think.'

'Oh. Really? Do you think so?'

'Haven't you noticed how happy she seemed after lunch, since Marcel said he would take up his apprenticeship?'

'Ah, you do have a knack of getting your own way. Where is he anyway? I've been looking for him all afternoon.' As the maid entered, he said, 'Laurence, has young Marcel turned up for tea yet?'

'No, Monsieur.'

'Hmm, where on earth can the lad be? He's not usually this late!' grumbled Monsieur Deforge while glancing at his pocket watch before passing into the garden with his wife.

Marcel swallowed down another lump of guilt. Guilt for the colony of insects pinned around the room. Guilt over Henriette, who would certainly take it badly if she knew his true feelings. But there was no point wallowing in it, he had to move on.

He belly-crawled under the door into the vast hallway. As he lifted his head on the other side, a brisk gust blew dust into his face. On rubbing his eyes, he caught the hem of Julia's dress as she moved away across the hall. That was all he needed. *What would she think of what she just heard?* he wondered. On the one hand, she looked quite put out, but that wasn't such a bad thing. On the other, she was going to think he had been lying to her.

'Come on, fellas, let's get a move on,' he called back to the crew.

To the right was the main entrance with its colonnaded porch, and straight across were the dining room, the scullery, and the kitchen to the rear.

The company followed suit over the smooth, cool surface of the black-and-white floor tiles. They inched along the skirting when in the open and travelled under furniture whenever possible, amid drifts of dust, knee-deep in places, where their trail bore witness to their passage. Crossing along the threshold of the main entrance was definitely a heart racer, especially when two great feet came plodding up and rubbed themselves diligently on the mat outside before attempting an entrance. Then at the last moment, they thankfully decided against it. The bookcase that sat against the dining room wall, on the other hand, proved an excellent run. It took them a whopping three full meters onwards in solid safety during which Marcel was asked to give further instruction as to the invisible walls.

'They can either let in air from outside or block it out while letting in its light. So if you can't smell the outside, it means the window is shut, and there's no point bumping yourself silly trying to get through it. See the window on the left? That's closed, and the one on the right is open. Even I can smell the air coming through it,' said Marcel, stepping out from under the bookcase to get some arm space. But just as he was pointing at the open window in question, there came a deep groaning sound, and he scuttled back in the nick of time, before a very large, dripping tongue lapped the very spot where an instant earlier he had been standing. 'Keep back!' whispered Marcel. The four-legged monster gave another groan and sniffed the area with its big black nose. But thankfully the animal had business elsewhere and was soon trudging on its way to the front door, which it nudged open just enough to squeeze through.

'Woah, was that a mop?' asked Brimstone.

'No, that was a dog,' said Marcel. 'With a moppy head I grant you; his name's Chico. He must have sensed me. I usually let him lick my nose, see. So we'd better be making tracks out of here before he comes back sniffing!'

Onward they marched around the room until at last they found themselves travelling under a chest of drawers along the wall between the dining room and the kitchen. A strong bleach-like smell suddenly sent Marcel's antennae quivering. This was immediately followed by the sight of another shaggy head that charged out in front of them and just as quickly drew back.

'*That* was a mop!' cried the boy. 'Double back!' he ordered as the shaggy monster again reared and retreated its head, devouring every speck and crumb in its path and leaving its scent behind in a wet caustic trail.

'Quick—through the dining room instead. The mop'll have already been in there,' he hollered between breaths, leading the sprint. The next moment the four creatures were hurling themselves under the dining room door, with the mop hot on their heels.

The dining room shutters were pulled together to shield against the sun while letting in a mellow light between the cracks. The windows were closed and rattled from time to time from the odd gust kicking in from outside, but inside all was still except for a couple of madcap flies that zoomed around the center of the room. Occasionally they buzzed off their orbit at full speed into the solid glass panes that refused to let them through. Now that she knew all about invisible walls, resting for a bite beneath the wrought-iron radiator, Bea gradually felt prone to a ticklishness in her belly. This speedily grew into convulsions of shrill laughter, as she and the rest of the company behind her joyfully watched the flies head-bashing the windowpanes with insistence. Until, that is, one of them settled on a neatly folded napkin dropped on the floor about a foot from the radiator. It swiveled its head and angrily hooted, 'Oy, whachoo laughing at, fatso?'

'I am laughing at a couple of dimwits bashing themselves stupid!' retorted the bee, who was no longer laughing at all.

'D'ya hear that, Zef? The fat bee thinks she's got a better idea.'

'Oh, do me a favor. She couldn't fly straight, let alone think straight!' said the other fly, who had just touched down on its pads after looping the loop.

'But she *has* got a nice pouch of pollen, and I *am* famished, aren't you? Come on, let's sort her out!'

Marcel stepped forward from under the radiator. 'Hang on! I'm sure she didn't mean to offend,' he said.

'Oh, look, what 'ave we 'ere? Why it looks exactly like a biddy 'uman being. Call Mosqui over; she *will* be pleased!' said the fly.

'Hey, Mosqui, shake a leg and come and have a look what we've found for ya; dinner's come early!' called Zef.

Before Marcel could reply, there came a familiar high-pitched droning sound that in the evenings of late invariably induced a slap on the ankle, on the neck, or wherever it was he was having his blood pumped out of him by a mosquito. This ordinarily gave him only minor discomfort, but in his present state, it would probably leave him half vampirized. And sure enough, as the flies whizzed around, hassling Bea with their sifting trunks, Marcel turned in time to face the mosquito coming at him in unpredictable flight. She headed the charge with her long trunk from which emerged a terrifying apparatus consisting of two pairs of pointed blades and a pair of tubes for injecting and sucking. Marcel dived and rolled at the last instant to avoid getting jabbed, while the rhino and the inchworm rallied to the bee to shoo away the flies from around her baskets. The mosquito loop-the-looped and was soon homing in again on the fresh blood flowing beneath Marcel's soft skin.

The mosquito's flight was deceiving, and realizing that counting on dodging its razor-sharp blades was a high-risk option, he instead sprinted for cover beneath the napkin where he pulled a stiff flap of cotton over him for 360° protection. Moments later the serrated blades were dipping into the cloth above where the boy lay flattened against the floor. Luckily the napkin's fold reached up just far enough to keep him from being stabbed. But Marcel's refuge was to be but a short respite.

Behind the nerve-racking buzz, he made out the doorknob being turned, followed by footsteps, which halted at Marcel's temporary cover. The next moment the shelter was being lifted away to reveal the walrus moustache of Monsieur Deforge, who then placed the fallen napkin back in its dish on top of the radiator. Again the mosquito was right behind the boy, all blades showing, when suddenly there was a rapid swish of air and a splat. The mosquito was swatted.

'That's one less!' said Deforge, flicking the limp creature from swat to floor. Now that the immediate danger had passed, drained by both effort and emotion, Marcel stood still and looked up, fully exposed to Monsieur Deforge, in a plea for a hand out of the fix he found himself in. Deforge squinted right down at him, at first with curiosity and then with a look of disgust, which was soon blacked out by a huge shoe sole hurtling down upon him. The boy threw himself to the ground as the wooden floor shuddered and the light was instantly killed out. Deforge was about to bend down to observe the thing he had stamped on, laying beside the splattered mosquito, when the voice of Julia diverted his attention.

'Uncle, Aunty wishes to know if we ought begin tea before it gets cold.' Deforge stood upright, reached for his spectacle case on the radiator, and walked out of the room, grumbling through his moustache.

'All right, all right, I'm coming, even if nobody else will!'

13
Henriette's Secret

The bee, the inchworm, and the rhino stood word-less under the radiator with all eyes on the inert human body in front of the twitching mosquito.

'Marcel?' said the rhino at last in his soft baritone voice.

'We failed him for a measly basket of pollen,' said the bee.

But before the tender-hearted creature could break out into a sob, the boy suddenly exclaimed, 'And there'd better be some left; I could eat a horse!' He was as much amazed to be alive as the others were at seeing him pick himself up off the ground, perfectly unscathed.

'Hah, you could always start with the mosquito!' said Rhino in a considerably lighter tone of voice than usual.

'Marcel, thank goodness,' shrilled Bea, while he stepped over and plucked a flake of rose pollen from her basket.

'The arch of the shoe must have come over me instead of the sole. Lucky he wasn't wearing his glasses!'

'I'd say lucky the twee made you gwow so small; any bigger and you'd have been as sure a goner as the mosquito!' said Brim, which gave Marcel pause to ponder. With all his adventures, he had not actually been able to think much about why he had been shrunk.

'Yes, I s'pose if I hadn't, I would have been crushed under that foot all the same, though I wouldn't have escaped under its arch!' said Marcel, who realized that whatever the forces that had invoked his conscience, whatever the forces that had set him the present challenge, they were giving him strength and faith in his own aptitude while making him see he was in danger of walking into a life he was not meant for.

'What happened to the flies anyway?' asked Marcel, noshing down more pollen.

'Oh, they zipped out the door as soon as it was opened,' said Rhino, having a chew, too, and added, 'though not without getting their hooters knocked slightly out of joint first!'

Their little snack was suddenly interrupted by another rattle of the porcelain doorknob. With their portions of pollen, the four creatures scampered well underneath the radiator as the door opened. Marcel recognized two large feet when the skirt that was draped over them was raised slightly to allow them to swiftly stride across the room where the windows were pulled open.

'Where can he be? He's never normally late for tea. Oh, God, if he doesn't come soon, I think I shall die!' Marcel's heart suddenly sank. His determination floundered on hearing Henriette's fretful voice as the shutters were thrust outward to open the view of the shaded driveway that led to the east gate.

Clad in a taffeta dress of Russian green adorned with russet guipure of the color of her hair, she strode around the table, clasping her hands. 'He might have had an accident, a nasty fall, perhaps. Oh, my love, my sweetheart, it's so cruel to love and not be able to shout it out loud!' she uttered in an effort to contain her outburst.

He had no idea she was that smitten. How could he tell her he could no longer become her prince now? Suddenly there came a rumble of voices from the hall.

'Ah, I wonder who that is? Silly me, he's probably entered by the main drive,' she murmured, straining an ear. She cleared her throat, prodded her chignon, then strode back to the door where she dropped her skirt over her large feet and passed back into the hallway.

Marcel turned to his friends in despair. 'Talk about desperate, did you hear?'

'I 'eard all right, but I didn't understand head nor tail of her jabber, did you?' said Rhino, turning to Miss Bea.

'No, I don't speak human talk, either.'

So Marcel related his predicament of how to tell Henriette he did not share her feelings without hurting her.

'So you see?' he concluded some minutes later. 'I mean, if I let her down now, she might go and do something silly.' But before anyone could give an answer, a different pair of steps clicked into the dining room.

The person making them glided swiftly to the open window. She was wearing a high collar and a white serge dress drawn in at the waist. 'Marcel!' called Julia over the lawn, and then brought her head back in disconsolately. 'Marcel, where are you hiding?' she said in a softly defiant voice, leaving him drunk on her words and no longer able to resist a reply. He stepped out from under the radiator.

'I'm here, Julia,' he called out.

She turned round from the window and under her breath she said, 'What are you playing at? You say you want to get on, and yet my aunt says you're still due to start here at Villeneuve.'

'I'm not playing, Julia. It was planned that way before we met.'

'If what you told me was true about wanting to make your own way in the world, you would let it be known.'

'I just need more time to explain to Henriette.'

'Or is that why you're avoiding me?' Julia bit her knuckle at the thought.

'I'm not avoiding you. Julia, in fact, I think I—'

'Well if you don't tell them that you're sending your acceptance, then I shall ask you this: are you a profiteer, or a coward? In either case, Marcel Dassaud, I shall wish never to see you again!' she said, stamping her heel and stalking back across the room.

'Julia, Julia, I...I...please wait,' pleaded Marcel, as she glided as tall as a tower past him and out of the room.

'So that was your mate, was it, Marcel? Anyway, there's no use shouting,' said Brim, crawling up to his shoulder, 'she can't hear you. You're too small.'

'Oh. You mean she didn't hear a single word I said?'

'Not a word.'

'She called me a jitter-belly.'

'My feminine intuition tells me she might not be altogether wrong, Marcel,' said Bea reprovingly.

'Surely you can see my predicament, though? Besides, Henriette is counting on me.'

'I say nip the confusion in the bud, else if you let it bloom, the flower will be wasted forever, as much for her as for yourself!' said Miss Bea prudishly.

'Blasted Deforge; it's all his fault. How could I have been so dumb?'

'Oh, I don't think you're as dumb as you look, Marcel. Pewhaps you thought it was in your intewest, eh?'

Marcel could not counter Brim's supposition before the doorknob was turned again, and the large feet, this time considerately lighter, skipped into the room. They were followed by an even larger male pair of shoes that had a tendency to turn inward, and Marcel recognized them as belonging to the ungainly Wilfried Delpech. The door was softly closed; the feet skipped a few steps and touched each other at the end of the table.

'I thought you'd never come,' said Henriette with a ring of mirth in her voice that Marcel never knew she had.

'What with Father Brulin's gout, I thought we'd never get away. I was hoping, though, we'd miss tea; I can't stand it. Still, I would drink a barrel of it a day if I knew each time we could be together.'

'Oh, Wilfried, you do brighten up my day.'

'Henriette, but a day is too short; I long to brighten up your whole life.'

'I love it when you speak like that,' said Henriette excitedly.

'Have you still not spoken to your father?' said the scout on a darker note, straightening his glasses with one hand, as per his habit whenever he approached a delicate matter.

'No, I…I can't seem to get it out.'

'You know I wanted to get things straight before your birthday.'

'But we must proceed gently, step by step. You see, he has always spoken about me and Marcel, ever since we were found playing at prince and princess together in my bedroom when we were kids.'

'That's ridiculous, my little Riette—'

'Yes, I never ever wanted to be a princess. But I think he's always been afraid I wouldn't marry at all, and he's hinged everything on bringing us together. I admit I wasn't opposed to it, in fact I don't think I gave it much of a thought until you came along.'

'Then we'll just have to elope!'

'You can't ask me that, my love. My parents would die of grief and us of hunger.'

'But neither can you sacrifice yourself, nor our love, for childhood pranks, a father's whim, and a young upstart's bid for a patron to give him a head start in life!'

'That's unfair, Wilfried. I don't think that is Marcel's intention at all. He has enough talent to go it alone, you know; my father said so himself.'

'Then why don't you speak to Marcel about us? About your true feelings?'

'And why didn't you come along before? Anyway, it's awkward. He might do something silly. If only he were more grown up, I could speak to him, but he is so sensitive. I don't want to lose a dear friend, do I? Besides, there's no hurry.'

'But there is, don't you see? Your father celebrating Marcel's apprenticeship at your birthday is his way of bringing you officially together.'

'Just give me a little more time, *mon amour.*'

'No, Henriette, as of Saturday, Marcel has a pretext to see you every day and I none. My love, I might not be much of a match in your father's eyes, but if you don't at least let me try to say something this evening, then I shall take it that my love for you is worthless. And in that case, I'll have no choice but to take the cloth, as I was planning before we met, rather than suffer the risk of you slipping through my fingers. My nerves wouldn't take it,' said Wilfried with feeling while cradling Henriette's hands, when suddenly the door swung open and in walked Julia.

'Henriette! Wilfried! Oh, I didn't realize you were...together. I thought...well, never mind, it doesn't matter,' said Julia quite astonished, delighted, and intrigued to see the young lovers clasping each other's hands. In a flash, it all became clear why Henriette had become so attached to her piano and had kept Julia out of her private lessons. She was simply in love and ferociously keeping her lover to herself and, by consequence, her piano, too.

'Well, you know now. Promise not to utter a word,' pleaded Henriette.

'Of course I won't, but I think you ought to have a word yourself with your mother and father. They've already got you signed up with Marcel!'

'She won't say anything because she's scared of what Monsieur Deforge will say about my origins.'

'That's not true, Wilfried! I just need time to put it to him.'

'I know I'm hardly what you'd call well-born, but if I'm not good enough for you now, I never will be,' said Wilfried in his deep voice of reason, taking advantage of the unexpected spectator to further defend his cause.

'He's right, Henriette,' said Julia. 'It's time you took control of your life. I don't know what's gotten into you, or Marcel for that matter. Come on, having a rebellious fit is all a part of youth. And Wilfried, don't think for a second you're inferior just because your parents are honest farm workers.' Just then the voice of Deforge bawled out in the hall. 'Talk of the devil. Well, there's no time like the present,' said Julia, and with a nod of encouragement, she escaped through the door leading to the kitchen before Deforge swung open the door of the dining room. Henriette quickly swept to the window before the door was fully ajar.

'Yes, but they pollinate the flowers. Malzac says they're the farmer's best friends,' she said to Wilfried, as if to continue a conversation.

'Ah, there you are, Delpech. I do wish you'd stop stealing him away, my dear; he hasn't finished his tea. I was going to speak about the new machine we've been building.'

'He wanted to show me the bee nest, father.'

'Well, actually, sir, the truth is I have something important to say to you,' said the scout, straightening his glasses.

'Out with it then!' honked Deforge.

'I…er…must say that Miss Henriette and I are… um…are at a discordance—'

'Oh?' said Deforge. Behind his back, his daughter was imploring Wilfried with her eyes.

'Over the bees,' said the scout, finally yielding to her silent remonstrance. 'Yes, I think you'll agree that they will have outstayed their welcome if there is to be a gathering of guests, sir.'

'But Wilfried, I thought we'd agreed about giving them more time.'

'I'm sorry, Miss Henriette, I'm of the opinion they should go if you and Marcel are to hold your celebration this Saturday.'

'We'll just keep our distance, promise. I really want the bees to stay,' insisted Henriette with conviction. Of course, little to Deforge's knowledge, though her mouth was saying *the bees* her mind was picturing *Wilfried*.

'Well, perhaps you could give it until tomorrow, but then I think it would be wise to call it a day and call in a beekeeper and send them packing once and for all. Though I must admit, dear Miss Henriette, as a nature lover myself, it would hurt me more deeply than you could ever imagine to see them go.'

Marcel, still standing by the radiator, could hardly believe his ears as a muddle of feelings turned them scarlet. On the one hand, embarrassment—how dare she insinuate he was immature and sensitive, and if she was so grown up, why didn't she face up to her father herself? And on the other, shame—how could he have been so blind as to think she was ever counting on one day going out with him, let alone being his 'princess'? And then, liberation—all he had to do was tell Deforge himself, and they would both be free from the shackles of their idiotic innocence.

Unable to keep his revolt pent up any longer, he cupped his hands and called out at the top of his voice to Monsieur Deforge that he no longer wanted to stay on at the house.

'He can't hear you, Marcel,' said Brim. 'You're too small, wemember? You still have to gwow up before you tell him anything!' But at least he had begun to blast it off his chest, and at last he felt he was truly moving in phase with his conscience.

'Yes you're quite right, Wilfried,' continued Monsieur Deforge with a glance through the window. 'Best play it safe; can't have our guests getting bees in their bonnets! We'll consider the lime tree as out of bounds from now until I get the beekeeper over tomorrow to smoke 'em out.'

Marcel gave a gasp and lost no time in translating Deforge's last words. These left Bea fretting for home and family and Rhino to solemnly declare, 'I only hope we can get you to the royal jelly in time, Marcel.'

'Come on, Rhino, it's not that far now. We only have to get across the lawn to the driveway. And don't worry, Bea, once I get back to my normal size, I'll speak to the big, fat man, and the nest will be saved,' he said in a bid to revive their spirits. However, instead of the desired effect, they all pulled a terrified face and shrilled Marcel's name in unison.

But it was too late; he didn't stand a chance. A pig-hair brush softly swept him clean off his feet from behind into the enamel dish used ordinarily to gather breadcrumbs from the table. The next thing he knew, he was being transported at a horrifying height toward the open window.

'There,' said Deforge, 'the ghastly creatures get everywhere!' And he tossed the contents of the dish clean out of the window, which for Marcel was like being thrown off the second floor of the Eiffel Tower.

14
Airborne

He tumbled through the air amid a sprinkling of breadcrumbs and a dead mosquito. At least the fall would bring an end to all his troubles. He shut tight his eyes in expectation of the last thud. That thud came in mid-prayer but not as he had figured, more like hitting a feather bed.

If his lucky star had kept a pretty low profile during his lifetime, it shone down like a sun today. After lying still a few moments in fear of being in eternity, he at last opened his eyes to discover the sky filling the space above him and sheep-like clouds scurrying by.

While he had been crossing the house, the weather had started to turn. Legions of thunderclouds were now balancing on the Quercy Ridge that flanked the plain to the north and were threatening an assault. The mowed grass on the prairie was being tossed and turned, as if by invisible pitchforks, while the fresh smell of moisture in the air meant it must have already rained somewhere not far away. Another roll of distant thunder made Marcel's antennae bulge at their base and the tin pail he now found himself inside rumble.

Turning over his hands, he felt the sponge he had landed on, which occupied half of the bottom of the tin pail. He had little time, though, to thank his lucky star, as he recognized the singing voice of Laurence the maid, who then promptly picked the bucket up.

Getting up on his hands and knees on the bouncy surface of the sponge, it sunk in that he would probably have to go it alone from now on. Yet at the same time, in another part of his brain, something told him that if he did, he could be found guilty of betrayal. Was it not he who had led the company into the house with the promise of guiding them out again? But after a moment's tossing the divergent notions back and forth in his mind, he remembered telling them about windows, walls, and doors, which gave him enough matter to console his conscience. So he decided he would trust them to find their own way and wait for them at the foot of the lime tree.

Besides, right now he did have more pressing matters at hand. For starters, if the clouds in the evening sky were anything to go by, he had better find shelter quick or risk drowning in a puddle.

But how to get out of the bucket? It was suddenly put down with a clunk, which sent Marcel rolling off the sponge onto the tin floor. The clamorous squeak and creek that followed above made his heart leap into his larynx. Glancing up, he realized that the downpour would probably come sooner than expected, and sometimes in life it never rains but pours.

His horrified eyes were now filled by the dark gaping spout of the water pump. He instinctively bounded from tin floor to sponge as the first roaring deluge gushed out onto the far side of the bucket, instantly sopping that end of the sponge and making the part Marcel was on rise under the counter weight.

Still, every cloud has a silver lining, he thought, in the knowledge that the sponge would rise with the water level and, with a bit of luck, allow him to get within hopping range of the rim. There was one hiccup, though, to this scenario: with every booming cascade, the spongy raft was becoming more and more waterlogged. To add to this, the sponge itself was treacherously drawing up water. Now the springiness of the dehydrated sponge was essential for a decent hop-off. Marcel knew that if he waited too long, it would be as good as trying to hop out of a bog. He remained, clasping onto the driest corner of the raft as far back from the spray as he could, estimating that in another couple of pumps he would be close enough to leap to the rim. What to do if he got there, he dared not think.

'Come on, Laurence, what you waiting for?' he yelled, still squatting in expectation of the next torrent. There came the squeak but no creak. This could only mean that the pump had been halted in mid-movement, while in the bucket, the water was irrepressibly hydrating Marcel's square of dry land.

'Plums? All right, won't be a mo',' called the maid, apparently in answer to a beckoning hand somewhere out there. She then turned her shoulders full back into the pump lever, and a tremendous trunk of water went crushing into the sponge at the submerged end. The cascading counterweight made the soggy raft rise up clear of the water level at Marcel's end. He knew at once such a chance would not come twice. So he flexed his knees and, with the upward movement, shot up in an awesome leap worthy of any prairie hopper toward the lip of the tin pail.

Yet, in horror, he quickly realized he would be half a centimeter short of the target. Thankfully, though, at the point of midair suspension, he managed to slam his palms full on the tin wall and walk them up the rest of the way to the rim. He heaved himself astride, while Laurence intermittently continued her toil above him.

'Now what?' said Marcel. He could hardly be expected to just shove himself off into the precipice; his human bones would be smashed to smithereens and his skin split like a splattered grape.

Yet, in a few moments, Laurence, who was picking Reine Claude plums from the nearby tree, would soon be bound for the house with the bucket of water. There he was in two minds whether to hitch a bucket ride astride the rim or to risk a slide down the handle from where he could hop onto a neighboring branch when a voice trilled in his ear.

'You'll have to jump!'

'Gallfly!' cried Marcel. 'But it's too high!'

Just as he said this, his entire being was seized by an instinctive impulse that made him curve his head over his thorax in a nymphal pose and flex the upper back muscles. His jacket ripped in the middle, revealing two veined wings, which then shot out and unfurled.

'Now spread your wings! They're still soft, but they will hold your weight,' said the gallfly at length. Just as the bucket was about to be lifted away, with a new instinct, Marcel kicked back his legs, deployed his wings, and plunged headfirst into the gusty air.

The airborne maneuvers that followed left the boy in a state of hair-raising rapture, with his taught wings hugging the wind as he carved his way between bamboo shoots, narrowly missing one or two. He glided on another meter until at last he made a running landing before a cluster of clover.

'Wow, d'ya see that? I can fly!' exclaimed Marcel, catching his breath.

'Yes, you've certainly evolved since we last met. You landed on your feet this time!' said the gallfly, who had softly settled to Marcel's side. 'They aren't flappable wings though, so you must use them wisely, cause they won't give you any extra lift if you get preyed on.'

With the irksome notion of his continued metamorphosis sinking in, Marcel braved a peek over either shoulder at the brownish gliding apparatus rooted in his back.

'Evolved? To tell the truth, Gallfly, I don't know if I'm pleased to have them or not. And what about these bristles and these antennas?'

'Oh, I think you look stunning, much more… complete than before. You'll soon be wondering how you ever got on without them. I told you you'd end up fitting in.'

'This is what you call fitting in? You didn't tell me I was gonna metamorphose into an insect!'

'You can always eat some royal jelly; then everything will fall away with your moult...as long as you don't get eaten before. You still have plenty of time, you know—another two moons.'

'No, I haven't,' said Marcel, who seated himself on a twig and, fiddling with an antenna with one hand and giving shape to his thoughts with the other, explained about the bees' imminent departure.

This prompted the gallfly to respond, 'As long as you've still got your will!' Marcel stopped fiddling and returned a flummoxed look at the gallfly's simplicity of statement as she continued, 'You have still got it, haven't you?'

'Well, yes.'

'There you are, then. There is a way, isn't there?' she concluded, quite self-satisfied with her effort to appease a distraught mind and then added, 'Do you know you're becoming a garden celebrity? Everyone's talking about you and your team, you know.'

'My team?'

'Yes, where are they, by the way?'

'Well, I've, er, had to break out ahead alone, actually,' said Marcel, stroking an antenna.

'Don't tell me; I bet they've dropped you for a ripe bush, especially the inchworm.'

'No, actually, we got split up crossing the house.'

'Bligh, that must have been risky. Then they left you behind, typical! Never mind, you mustn't hold it against them; they probably lacked courage, Marcel, cause it sometimes takes great courage to stand by friends when the going gets tough, doesn't it?'

'Actually, they're still in the house, I was about to—'

Suddenly a streak of lightening lit up the sky, closely followed by a booming crack of thunder, so saving Marcel from telling a lie.

'Oh dear,' said the gallfly nervously, 'I'd rather be off before the darkness thickens. I've never flown in the dark before, you know, and I must admit I haven't the slightest bit of will for doing so, and even less courage, so I'll be seeing you.'

Marcel bid the little creature good-bye as the storm continued to surf around the Quercy Ridge. A flash of lightening and crack of thunder hit at one point simultaneously overhead, but as of yet, no rain fell on the plain where Villeneuve stood snuggled safe and sound amidst its wooded grounds. Nevertheless, the rich hues of the afternoon were precociously dissolving, each stitch in the tapestry of light being gradually gobbled up by the encroaching gloom, which lent a sullen air to the pre-evening. Marcel lapsed a moment into the well of end-of-day melancholy known to man, wolf, and cicada and, feeling quite alone and scared, though he would not have admitted to this, began missing his crew. Perhaps the gallfly was right; it is sometimes easy to abandon friends though probably more courageous not to. So despite the announced downpour, despite the loss of precious time he would incur, he resolved to recover his motley crew.

15
The Localola Flower

'Well, Father Brulin, if you are quite sure you'll not wait until the storm has passed.'

'No, no, God bless you, Monsieur Deforge. I bet it's going to be a dry one anyway; it is often the case, you know. If there's no north wind to push it down across the plain, you can be sure it'll follow the ridge round and shed what's left of its load over Mirabel.'

'That is true. They're often the lucky ones. My farmer will be grumbling again,' chuckled Deforge, while showing the curé out of the house.

'Anyway, I'll speak to the beekeeper tomorrow and get young Wilfried to bring him along for you. Say around teatime after the heat has relented?'

'That would be fine, thank you, Father.'

'Come along Wilfried, give us a leg up.'

Wilfried had pulled up nag and carriage before the porch and was now climbing down to help the old parish priest up. Henriette was standing behind her father, between the two Corinthian columns of the porch in the glow of the all-new electric lantern above her. As soon as Father Brulin's back was turned, she blew a quick imploring kiss, which Wilfried, despite his sullen look, discreetly caught, kissed, and sneaked inside his blazer. Henriette was well under cupid's spell; it had the effect of rounding her usually long face, thought Marcel who, comparing her shapely body with the vertical columns, suddenly saw that he was not the only one metamorphosing at Villeneuve.

He had just landed and let his wings retract on his back after deploying them alternately with hops. He was standing on the edge of the trim turf that bordered the bare ground of the driveway, no more than half a dozen meters from the porch. The old horse with its buggy was soon clopping past the windswept cedar into the alley of horse chestnut trees. Monsieur Deforge ushered his daughter into the house where the cheery artificial light from the lantern was struck out.

The powerful daytime song of the cicada had long since ceased. And though the familiar evening litany of grasshoppers and crickets was music to his ears, a whole new soundscape of eerie noises seemed to creep up with the encroaching darkness. Marcel got the feeling he was being watched. His heart pounded in his chest when he was sure something appeared over his shoulder and brushed against his ear. Knife at the ready, he turned quickly to catch whatever it was in the half-darkness, expecting to come face-to-face with the vole. Until, that is, he realized the fleeting movement in the tail of his eyes was none other than himself, or more precisely, his wings. Their presence gave him more cause for worry than comfort, however. But a second later, an appalling crash of thunder shook him in his boots, prompting him to get set for another series of hops and glides, this time across the driveway to the porch, when suddenly he heard someone.

'Hey, dude, don't do it!' sang out a kind of vibrant musical voice that belonged to a hovering creature that closely resembled a wasp.

Marcel's antennae gave a hesitant twitch, leaving him unsure as whether to halt in mid-step or to hop it.

'Stay cool, dude. I ain't what you're thinkin'. Looky here; ain't no stinger stickin' out of my butt! Nope, I'm a hoverfly,' quavered the insect, waggling his dartless abdomen as living proof.

It then alighted on a cloverleaf and continued. 'Yep, a fly in wasp's clothing, that's what I am. I get to hang out in places any other fly wouldn't even dream of, and the birds, no sweat, man. See, I'm like permanently under cover. My friends call me Le Camouf, by the way, as in Camouflage.'

'My name's Marcel,' offered the boy, gradually be-coming reassured by the insect's affable nature.

'Marcel? *The* Marcel? Oh, Holy Mother! Like the Marcel who outsmarted the snake? The Marcel who made mincemeat out of the mosquito? Gee whiz, wait 'til my buddies hear about this!' said the hoverfly whose overstatements Marcel chose to pass over for fear of spoiling the creature's manifest pleasure.

Moreover, it is fair to say that Marcel was not in-sensitive to the thought of becoming a garden celebrity overnight, though, of course, modesty obliging, he tried not to show it. But the young man had much to learn about body language. His antennae that now swept back on the sides of his head in a totally disarmed manner betrayed the secret of his gratification as good as if he had beamed a smug smile.

'Oh, been in a few scrapes, I s'pose.'

'What were ya gonna jump out there for?'

'My friends are inside the house.'

'Peuf, it just goes to prove that even the smartest can come to a stupid end.'

'What do you mean?'

'I mean, lucky for you I showed up. See, even you can't hop across that driveway!'

'Why's that?'

'Cause that land is sick land. Looks all right, smells all right, but you touch it, and you will get contaminated; you will die, Marcel. In less than a single moon, you will be as cooked as a slug in the midday sun!' said Le Camouf the hoverfly, emphatically hammering out the syllables from the top of the flowering clover.

It occurred to Marcel that Malzac often sprayed weed killer over the drive in a continued campaign to maintain frontiers. This must be the reason for that land being so 'sick,' he thought.

'And besides that,' added the hoverfly, pointing back across the trim expanse of dark green turf toward an even darker thicket of vegetation, 'you ought to be heading that way for shelter. Can't you tell it's gonna rain? The last time it came down, I got hit by a blob. I was stuck in it for ages.'

'On the contrary,' said Marcel, holding his chin, as would any self-respecting connoisseur about to dispense some of his science, 'there'll be no rain on the plain to-night.'

'Oh, and what makes you say that?'

'Look, the wind's coming from that direction (*he pointed to the west*), pushing the clouds away in that direction (*he pointed to the east*), listen!' And with uncanny timing, there came a deep roll of thunder grumbling away easterly along the Quercy Ridge.

'Well, would ya get that? They said you had *some* brainpower, dude, and I do believe them! And now you mention it, I can smell it is getting fainter. How did you figure that?'

'Human knowledge,' said Marcel, mysteriously tapping his temple with an index finger.

'And what the toad's warts is knowledge?' asked the hoverfly, playing it dumb, which Marcel, who was coveting hopes of a boost in his celebrity ranking, failed to see.

'In other words, I put previous observations together and, well, the thought came to me,' he said.

'You mean it just popped into your head? Wow, Holy Mother, with brainpower like that, buddy, why I'd be in danger of ruling the world!'

'Anyway, before you start thinking of ruling the world, if you could just tell me how I can get to my friends in the house?'

'How do you know they're still in there, first? I mean, I hate to say so, Marcel, but they might have been eaten already, or squashed or gassed or who knows. Or they might have just plain gotten out by now for all you know.'

It was true enough, thought Marcel. 'But they *are* my friends. We've been through a lot together; I hate to think of them stuck in there.'

'Ah, you'll find others,' said Le Camouf. The moment he said this, he quite unexpectedly stood bolt upright, casting a horror-struck gape upwind along the drive past Marcel's shoulder. 'Woahhh!!' he shrieked, as he took to the air. 'Run for it, Marcel. This way!'

Marcel turned in time to catch a glimpse at a great brown thing the size of a river rat scurrying like the wind straight at him from the shadows.

'Hop this way,' cried the hoverfly, buzzing before the lad and toward the thicket of vegetation.

With the flurry of wind behind his wings, Marcel managed to throw himself high into the air and glide a full two meters over the grass. His landing, though technically speaking less successful, was no less spectacular. For the force of the wind threw him off balance, making him tumble onto his knees and follow through into a commando roll. And just as well it did, too; a second later the brownish unidentified bounding object went bouncing barely a centimeter clean over him before sailing on by in the tail end of the flurry until it faltered and came to rest a few meters further.

'It was only a flaming plane tree leaf!' said Marcel, picking himself up and quite rankled with it.

'Was it? Phew, close shave though, and didn't you make a dashing escape,' cheered Le Camouf in his usual good humor, which had the effect of tempering Marcel's annoyance. 'Come on, this way, just a bit further and there's some nice localola pollen,' he said in his cantering way amid the soothing sound of grasshopper songs coming from the thicket.

'But my friends might need me, and I definitely need a guide.'

'I'll be your guide. I can lead you to the royal jelly, even in the pitch darkness. And the best way's through the thicket and round the lily pond, come on I'll show you.'

'Who said anything about royal jelly?' said Marcel, whose suspicion had at last been roused.

'You didn't? Ah. Well, all right, I confess; I overheard the end of your conversation with the gallfly,' admitted Le Camouf, adopting an artfully awkward stance.

'And what would you want royal jelly for?' questioned Marcel, who was not so naïve as to think the hoverfly's proposal would come without compensation.

'Because if I ate some royal jelly, I figure I could become a real wasp, or even a hornet, with a real dart,' said Le Camouf, shrewdly meeting Marcel's suspicion

head-on, which was better than the young human getting wind of the hoverfly's true intentions. 'Then I could
do all my hunting for myself. See, I'm sick of living on
plain pollen and rotting carrion left over by the grasshoppers. I've got more ambition than that, you know.'

'So that's why you stopped me from jumping onto
the drive, is it?'

'Oh no, not only, Marcel. I knew you were the boy
wonder the moment I first set eyes on you. I wanted
you to be my precious friend so I could show you to my
mates, who could coach you in the art of getting into
the honeybee nest. Come on, Marcel, stick with me and
we'll both be getting lashings of gob-smacking metamorphosing royal jelly, trust me.'

The hoverfly's persuasive parlance gradually got
the better of Marcel's resistance. After all, it was true
that his companions could be anywhere by now, and
he had better get on. Soon he found himself travelling
down the lawn to the thick belt of vegetation that lay
before the lily pond where modulations of grasshoppers
seemed to be outsounding creaks of crickets and croaks
of tree frogs.

How he envied the hoverfly who, to quash his
impatience, had winged it there and back half a dozen
times by the time Marcel reached in laborious bounds
the edge of the thicket. For even on a well-trimmed
lawn, hopping and gliding is not as smooth a means of
travel as you might think. Without the fluttering facil-
ity of most flying creatures, Marcel was unable to land

gently. More often than not, through lack of a flat running space, he had no other option than to hurl himself onto grass blades or clover leaves whose springiness cushioned his landing.

But the greatest setback, which was also at times his greatest ally, was the wind. Though it had mostly died down, from time to time it kicked up in eddying squalls. On one occasion he found himself helplessly drifting around amid the stream of a whirlpool that set him down half a hop back from where he had taken off.

At last he landed at the edge of the thicket, where he sat down to catch his breath and gather his thoughts on a cedar twig that barred a vole-size passage leading into the dense vegetation.

To nourish his eyes, Marcel cast his gaze to the west, where the last dregs of daylight were fast evaporating, despite the sun beaming its rosy revenge between thinning clouds. And with the increasing darkness, across the neat and still lawn, he could now make out a slither of light that outlined the dining room shutters closed to the night. He pictured the house behind them having their evening meal with all the trimmings of civilization—a stark contrast to the dark passage behind him and the eerie sounds of fauna there within. All right, he had been through this shuddering business before and had vanquished his fear of the dark once already. But this time he had a strange feeling, different from plain fear. It was more like a foreboding that weighed on his mind now, and that was accompanied by a foul smell.

'Come on, Marcel. Can't stay 'ere forever, and there's no going back now. It's too dangerous to stay out in the open after nightfall,' said Le Camouf in his most vibrant voice. Anticipating the lad's uneasiness, he then added, 'The moon will be up shortly if the clouds move on as you said they would, and you'll feel better once you've got some localola pollen inside you.'

Still seated on the log-like twig, Marcel looked from the affable hoverfly to the dark passage, when his ears were alerted by a distant but familiar scratching coming from the glazed doors of the vast hall of Ville-neuve. On turning his head back to the house, he caught the short, dumpy silhouette of the maid opening one of them for the dog.

'Better get going; this is its favorite peeing ground,' said Le Camouf, pointing at the Pyrenean sheepdog, which for the moment luckily went off in another direction.

'Thanks for the info!' snapped Marcel, pulling a revolted face. He was, however, nonetheless privately reassured as to the probable origin of the vile smell. But what did most to quash his apprehension was the porch lantern being switched on, which splayed the thinnest film of light over the ground, all the way to the lily pond, and the remembrance that it had become Deforge's habit to leave the light on as a display of his modernity to the outside world, at least until bedtime.

So Marcel put his anxiety to the back of his mind, slipped over the cedar twig, and after being reassured that the vole had long since met with the cat, stepped into the dark, eerie passage behind the hoverfly, who led the way on foot. They toiled on along the beaten trail, where for want of space it was virtually impossible to hop. It led them past an array of pond-side plants and between densely growing papyrus and reeds that for Marcel shot up as tall as lighthouses. The faint glimmer from the porch lantern that touched the highest peaks made passing through the thicket of vegetation slightly less daunting. And as the thinning cloud straggled away, the stars began to sparkle more and more brightly as if they had been given a good shine.

Was it fatigue or was it hunger that seemed to lull his anxiety away? Or was it the constant purring that resounded in his ears all around? Yet he was constantly reminded that danger lay all about. Beneath the comforting modulations, from time to time, there came sudden outbursts, instantly followed by terrifying cries of creatures in the throes of agony and, yet, they had met no one along the way, at least not so far.

By now they must have travelled midway into the dark and dank thicket. Suddenly Le Camouf jumped into the air, hovered ten centimeters off the ground for a split second to get a better view, and whizzed back down. Without a word, he ushered Marcel off the vole track into the dark grove of papyrus that flanked it. The boy was about to demand an explanation when there came a snorting sound: sniffing and feeling its way up the trail came a massive black velvet creature with enormous paws that could only belong to a mole. The two stole silently away from the scene as swiftly as they could between the great stalks of the grove, whose density, thank goodness, forbade entrance to anything larger than a field mouse.

After a while they came to a small clearing in the middle of which stood a lone plant. It consisted of long, low-lying broad leaves forming a star shape that cupped a massive flower in the center that even in the feeble light beamed with splendor. The fragrant crimson petals were drawn down, revealing stamens bristling with pollen and a receptacle brimming with nectar. Marcel stood gazing at it an endless instant and wondered when he would awake from such a fantastical dream and find himself back under the oak tree where his extraordinary journey had begun. But he did not.

'That's the localola plant,' said Le Camouf in a low voice that Marcel hardly took note of. Was it hunger or thirst? the sight of abundance or the sweet smell of nectar that despite his apprehension drew Marcel like one possessed to the gigantic flower some twenty paces across the glade, amid the hypnotic song of grasshoppers?

'You not having any?' he asked, hardly able to mouth the words properly because of his taste buds fizzling all over his tongue. And without waiting for the answer, he reached into the flower and scooped up loving handfuls of pollen dust.

'You eat; I'll keep a lookout,' said the hoverfly, now perched on a leaf and visibly amused at the spectacle of the young human gorging himself. 'Besides, I had some just before we met,' he lied. 'That's how I know it's here. Lucky, too, come tomorrow it'll all be gone, so tuck in,' said Le Camouf, knowing full well that Marcel was past listening. 'But by then we should have you perfectly trained to fetch the royal jelly,' he said. With the young human at long last at the localola flower, Le Camouf could no longer resist giving vent to his design of gaining the loads of royal jelly needed to make the dream of owning his own dart come true. According to insect lore, large quantities of the regal food will induce extended metamorphosis, and the hoverfly needed a thief conditioned to get it for him. 'That's it; eat up. You'll be needing all your strength to bring us back plenty of the noble nectar!' he continued, excitedly rubbing his front paws together.

But, lost in his fervor, Marcel wasn't listening and proceeded to snap off a stamen, bite off one end, and use it as a straw to drink up the lip-smacking nectar like there was no tomorrow.

'Absolutely de-li-ci-oso; pity the others aren't here,' he slurred drunkenly after a long moment of noshing and sipping and lifted his head from the flower cup to motion to the hoverfly to join him. But the hoverfly was not there.

Now that he had stopped mashing, munching, and slurping, Marcel was able to perceive the ghostly silence that had fallen with the dead of night around him. His mind became suddenly chaotic, as it asked why the hoverfly had not joined in the feast, and why was it that the flower had not been touched before? Poison? The notion alighted on his mind at the same instant he sensed a chilling presence in his back. Groggy-headed, he turned. His blurry eyes met with the hoverfly, smiling and dwarfed before three green-armored creatures with powerful mandibles, huge bulbous eyes, and great spiny legs as his own legs gave way beneath him and he swooned to the ground senseless.

16
Trespassers Will Be Eaten

The porch lantern had long since been extinguished. Its feeble glimmer was now superseded by the brilliant light of the full moon that gleamed like a silver ecu in the purple sky; and there was no escaping it. It glistened in the lily pond where the frog took a gobbling leap. It crept upon the sleeping snail for the hedgehog to crunch. It cut out shadows for the owl to pounce on. And while the cautious cricket chirped its summer serenade just a stride from the safety of its burrow, the dozing cicada was rudely shaken from its sun-drenched dreams by the preying green grasshopper that savagely plunged its muzzle into the soft sap-filled belly for the choicest morsel. Indeed the night was made for the hunt. Another morbid cry of horrid surprise at last brought Marcel back to his senses, though his limbs were still half paralyzed in slumber.

In the pale light of the moon, he made great efforts to retrieve his arms from above his head—their position attested to his having been dragged to his present emplacement—but they might just as well have been cast in lead. At the same time, a grasshopper peered over him, making his heart thump like a drum in his ribcage.

'Kalif, it's coming round!' called the creature thickly, swiveling its stinking bloody head.

The biggest of the green grasshoppers left its feasting and appeared at Marcel's feet. His huge globular eyes peered into the boy's gaze. His smile was vile, as he affably said, 'Don't you know you are trespassing?'

'Trespassing?' stammered Marcel at the nightmarish gape. Though still quite dazed, he nevertheless had the presence of mind to search for something else to focus his eyes on, a lesson he had learnt from a previous occasion. Instead they fell upon a macabre scene behind the celadon green beast and in front of a bed of crimson hinged leaves, which Marcel recognized as belonging to a carnivorous Venus flytrap plant. There was the hoverfly, impatiently eyeing a grasshopper chomping into the belly of a cicada still twitching helplessly on the ground. Another awful cry suddenly broke out from the surrounding thicket.

'Trespassing. And trespassers are usually eaten!' pursued Kalif, the chief grasshopper, delectably rubbing his muzzle with his palps, while Marcel writhed on the quagmire floor. 'Spare your strength, Marcel. You are still under the effects of the localola plant. Besides, you need not fret, if you have come in friendship, all charges against you may be dropped. I personally have been looking forward to meeting you, you know, ever since young Alf sung of your quest before being *swallowed*, if you'll forgive the pun!' Kalif chuckled lordly.

The other grasshoppers guffawed, while Marcel recalled the grasshopper on the thistle flower.

'Hark, hark, another dozing cicada!' said Kalif, lending an antenna to yet another cry of dreadful surprise. Marcel, despite the black dread in his liver, writhed some more, like a larva on the sodden floor, and this time he felt his muscles beginning to loosen up. But his wrists were instantly clamped firm to the ground by two claws belonging to the first bloody-faced grasshopper, who loomed its lacerating jaws over the lad's belly.

'Is this how you welcome a friend?' said Marcel, trying his best to bolster his voice and nodding up to the fiend arresting his arms. The chief in turn gave a flick of the head to his acolyte, who instantly bowed off and let go. Discretely tensing his muscles, the lad found he was gradually regaining possession of them though took care not to move his limbs. He figured it best that these ghouls continued to think he was still half paralyzed, so he could make his escape if ever their vigilance slipped.

'You can never be too careful in these parts. It's a bug-eat-bug world, you know,' said Kalif almost apologetically, then with sudden force, he thundered with destabilizing effect, 'So you come in friendship, do you?'

'I come here meaning no harm,' returned Marcel humbly, resisting the urge of recoiling his body.

'Good,' encouraged the grasshopper more quietly. 'Then as a friend, tell us the secret of man's long life, and I will let you go. If you won't, then you are no friend of mine, and we shall have to find out for ourselves,' said the grasshopper while trying to pierce through Marcel's gaze.

Marcel racked his brain, sensing that his life would be worth no more than the gutted cicada lying on the mire floor if he did not come up with an answer of some sort. 'Er, it's in our physical composition,' he returned at last.

'In our what?' growled the grasshopper, lunging his head forward.

'I mean, we all have a kind of inner clock pertaining to our species that tells us when to eat, sleep, grow up, and die. Man's clock runs longer than a grasshopper's, that's all,' said Marcel nervously.

'A clock? Hmm. And where is this clock kept?'

'Well, no one can tell where it actually is, or what it looks like even—'

'You lie!'

'N...no, I...I...assure you, else everybody would be putting it back.'

'Hmm. Good news: I believe you, boy. Bad news: we're just going to have to search for ourselves.'

Kalif turned to the other grasshoppers. 'He must be talking about his thumper,' he said, then flicking out a claw, he boomed, 'Cut it out!'

Marcel was about to make a desperate appeal when the hoverfly stepped forward feverishly. 'Ang on, Kalif, that's not fair.' Marcel was momentarily heartened by the vibrant intervention, until the very next instant the hoverfly divulged his true intentions. 'We had a deal: I bring him to you, you put him under, he gets enough royal jelly for the both of us.'

'Stupid, it's not royal jelly I'm after. Now pipe down or buzz off,' said Kalif.

'But I found him; you gave your word. You can do what you like with him after—'

'Call me a rotten swindler if it makes you feel better, and we'll be two of a kind!'

'I've been looking forward to getting my dart,' said the hoverfly, getting really worked up.

'It wouldn't suit you. Now go fetch us some more refreshment and not too old this time. The last thing you brought in had bits in its belly!'

'Right, if you kill 'im before I get me royal jelly, then don't go counting on Le Camouf, the best puller on the patch, to lure your cockchafers and your cicadas so you can take it easy.'

'Oh, shut your trap!'

'I mean it, Kalif. Without the likes of me, you'll be eating grass for the rest of your days!'

'Shut him up!' Upon Kalif's lordly flick of a claw, the grasshopper seized the hoverfly and threw him into a gaping Venus flytrap leaf. He landed smack on the center fold of the leaf and lay there in terror an instant. But the plant made no move.

Le Camouf sprang back onto his feet and victoriously he jeered, 'Hey guys, hah hah hah, now come and get me!' Then cockily he jibed, 'You wait till I tell everyone—' But as he was about to take off, he slipped on the smooth waxed surface, knocked against a bristle, and the hinged death trap clapped shut, enclosing him. The more he struggled to desperately pry the leaf open, the more it closed around him, tighter and tighter, until he buzzed no more, and the plant released the digestive acids to begin the slow process of fluid extraction.

The grasshoppers stood gawking at the carnivorous plant with strange fascination, while Marcel, taking advantage of the current distraction, began to discretely roll away in what might be his only chance to escape.

His limbs were still pretty sluggish, but at least he could now shift them, and after the second roll, he decided that upon the next he would spring up and hop it. But on completing the third roll, four claws came down like iron shackles, clamping his outstretched limbs to the boggy ground and dashing all hopes.

Holding down the boy's ankles, Kalif rumbled, 'Who do you think you are?' and blazed his huge powerful eyes down at his miniature human trespasser.

The question ricocheted through Marcel's mind, bringing down barriers and wending its way to the profound quarters of his brain. Yes, who was he really? Where was he going? These were thoughts he had never much bothered with before. And though hardly the most appropriate moment to call them to mind, he felt impelled in that timeless instant to proceed with their exploration. Was he a boy, an insect, a young man? Was he real even? Would he reach the light his companions spoke about? Would he go to God or to Mother Nature? Would he go anywhere at all if his life came to an end now?

One thing he did know was that were he to live but another year, another month, another week, he would live it to the full. Nothing else now mattered, not fear of speaking his mind, nor ridicule, nor failure. He would no longer be scared to assert his talents, to forge his own way ahead, to make his mark on life. He would live as though it could all end tomorrow. That is what he would do were he to survive this nightmare.

'I am a young man,' he asserted with the full weight of Kalif's gaze upon him.

'Well, young man, you have a strong will, I grant you that. Now, last chance, tell me the secret of long life and you may go.'

'Staying away from grasshoppers is one!' Marcel retorted with new spirit.

'Flippancy doesn't suit you. Just answer the question!' thundered Kalif and flicked an eye to his counterpart pinning down the lad's wrists. The next instant, Marcel felt an excruciating pain, like an electric shock shooting through his head. The insect had severed an antenna.

'Ahhhh! I told you; it's all to do with our inner clock,' said Marcel, cringing under the pain.

'Tell us where it is, and I will let you go!'

'You're a liar! You won't let me go.'

'Shorten the other one!' The order was instantly executed.

'Ahhhh! No one knows where it is, and there is nothing you can do to steal someone else's from them, so there is no point trying. I told you the secret, now let me go!'

'I shall be the judge of that,' said the lordly creature. 'Cut him up, layer by layer. I want to see his inner workings. And I want his thumper in one piece,' he commanded, while Marcel, powerless to move, could only crush his fear under grit teeth as the third grasshopper placed its jaws on his jacket and began to snip away at his lapels, taking them for part of his person.

Kalif craned over the operation, beaming his huge eyes into the lad's gaze in an attempt to pry into his mind. 'We're going to make you eternally beautiful, eternally famous; your name will be passed on from generation to generation as the person who gave us longevity. So keep still and be grateful. Now look into my eyes; it will take away your suffering, honest,' he grinned.

Dissecting his blazer was, of course, no skin off the boy's nose, but his waning strength meant his resistance to Kalif was wearing thin. At length he felt himself being drawn into the spinning pools of the eyes that sat like blobs of puss on the grasshopper's head. Until from behind there came a loud lapping of water and the groan of a dog.

'Chico!' he muttered, at first more to take his mind off the ghoulish beasts around him than to attract the attention of the dog. He knew full well it would probably not hear him anyway. 'Chico, Chico!' he yelled.

The repetition of the name was like throwing out a mooring line to keep his mind from breaking adrift. 'Chico, Chico, Chico,' he screamed louder and louder, disturbing the delicate operation in progress.

And, against all odds, a heavy panting came closer and closer. Kalif, on the approach of the groaning quadruped, released his hold of the trespasser and glanced down with disgust at the summoner of the great hairy beast. He then exchanged a wide-eyed look of consternation at his fellow creatures, for the sheepdog was already upon them.

'Play dead!' Kalif snapped to his acolytes, as Marcel rolled his body from their midst. A second later Chico was cocking a leg over the very spot where Marcel had lain captive. The dog then trundled tranquilly on his way, apparently oblivious to the mayhem he had just caused. Marcel's torturers were drenched and dragging themselves from the puddle when suddenly there was a tremendous hullabaloo.

'Charge!' cried a litany of familiar voices. The three faithful companions had jumped from a hind leg of the dog as it had passed on its way. Rhino steamed in like a raging bull, Brim shuffled in, rough 'n' ready to clobber anything in his way, while Bea clawed at Marcel's shoulder and dragged him to the edge of the battle zone. She gave him some extra specially mixed nectar before spinning into the fight herself.

The boy's head was still ringing, but at least the numbness was leaving his body. Nevertheless, still too weak to bowl into battle, he managed to prop himself up against a lone papyrus stalk growing at the edge of a veritable plantation of Venus flytraps. These, he deduced, must be part of Madame Deforge's experimental plan to reduce the number of mosquitoes. Across the clearing in the white moonlight, he watched his companions in the force of their union laying into the two remaining waterlogged grasshoppers that with every thump spurted water from their spiracles. But Kalif, he soon realized, was not one of them.

Scarcely had the sickening thought flashed through his brain than his mutilated antennae twinged at a movement from behind a plant. And there suddenly appeared, three paces before him, the avatar of his worst nightmare.

'Boo!' said Kalif in his darkest humor, though it was clear the beast was in no mood for banter. Marcel, not wanting to excite the predator's thirst for the kill, rose slowly and moved blindly backward, keeping his eyes on the animal's jaws.

'Did you think I'd run off like a thief without saying good-bye? Oh, no, I wouldn't do that, especially as I left you with something very precious, remember? Now, that clock. Tell me where you keep it; it will save us both time,' continued the grasshopper.

It was pointless calling for help; his friends were busy, and even if they did hear him, he would most certainly be dead by the time they got to him. Instead, trying not to lose his head, he decided his only option was to keep the grasshopper talking until something came up, and so he said, 'Why do you want to live such a long life, Kalif?'

'Because I happen to like it!' snapped the grasshopper.

'I mean, I thought every insect wanted to reach Mother Nature's light.'

'Rubbish! I have other ambitions. Do you think it fair that only humans can improve their condition?' he pleaded while again trying to pin down Marcel's gaze with his eyes, though this time the lad resisted. 'Give me time and I will rule these lands!' said the predator in contained wrath while moving forward in time with Marcel's backward steps, like some macabre foxtrot. Slow, slow, quick, quick, slow, between the sinuous path they went with the grasshopper expounding his plan of how he would escape his condition and become master of the destiny of his kind.

Meanwhile, the boy, promptly becoming cornered between three carnivorous plants, had no choice but to clamber between the treacherous leaves that resembled great eyes with long lashes. Marcel in the past had lain down and observed such leaves as these a hundred times and never ceased to marvel at the plant's mechanism of extracting fluids from the living. He knew it did not close over its prey intentionally, at least not like a human thought, more like a bear trap in that pressure had to be applied on a trigger. And that trigger could be any one of the half a dozen thorn-like bristles that sprouted over the surface of the leaf, each one with the capacity to activate the trap once only before becoming a dud.

This was the tenor of Marcel's thoughts as Kalif, in slow deliberate movements, climbed after him. 'You see, Marcel,' he said drawling his words smugly, 'I notice things other insects wouldn't even suspect. With my powers of observation and your longevity, I am destined to become the lord of this land. And my offspring will venerate me as the first to break out from the condition of good old Ma Nature. See these sweet-smelling plants, for example. One false move and—snap—it's got you,' he said and slipped a long leg over an open Venus flytrap leaf, touched a bristle, and quickly pulled it out again before the leaf closed shut like a clam. 'You see? I sussed that out for myself,' he said proudly. 'Many more things I know and will have time to learn now with your help. Why else would you have fallen into my path?'

Now in the thick of the plantation of carnivorous plants, Marcel's backtracking space was becoming more and more hampered with the deadly two-faced leaves. But that made little odds against him, for he was certain that the grasshopper, in his mad misconception, was on the verge of leaping for his throat anyway. The boy knew he must strike first to stand a chance, and better sooner than later, for in two more steps, Kalif would have his back to a large open leaf.

'I haven't come here for you, Kalif,' he returned, punctuating the chat.

'That is where you are wrong. I will do great things with your longevity. What would you do with it, hmm? Grow up, grow old, and wither away. That's hardly much to live for, is it? A perfect waste of good time, if you ask me. By giving yourself up, you will be partaking in a great step of grasshopper evolution.'

'All right then, Kalif, you can take this for starters,' retorted Marcel, ripping off a shred of his lapel, which he hurled to one side of the bemused grasshopper in order to create a diversion. And, summoning all his strength and courage, the boy leapt at the grasshopper, hurtling his feet toward the powerful mandibles. But Kalif was no dupe, at the last moment, he deflected the flying kick, leaving Marcel, instead of bounding off the predator with his feet, crashing his upper body into him, which sent them both toppling onto the surface of the Venus flytrap leaf.

But the plant did not bat an eyelid. Thankfully the bristle they landed on must have been a dud. The grasshopper had already grabbed hold of Marcel's leg, and a second later would have been ripping into the boy's throat like an enraged lion if Marcel had not yelled, 'Move and we both die, Kalif!'

Kalif twitched a terrible eye at his human prey and stopped dead. The sight of the lad holding a bristle brought him out of his blind fury and, realizing where he had landed, shifted his eyes over the expanse of the leaf in the middle of which lay a mangled and withered two-winged corpse.

'Let go, Kalif, else I'll trigger the trap!' said Marcel, careful not to look directly into the grasshopper's eyes.

'I'd be careful there, Marcel. It will be a slower death if you do,' said the insect, retracting his claws from Marcel's breaches. 'What do you suggest we do then, sit here all night long, telling each other stories?'

Marcel, now having recovered the full fluidity of his mind, came up with an idea he might have used before had he been in full possession of his faculties. He reached into his inner pocket and, pulling out his timepiece, said, 'Here, this is my clock. It is set to man's time; it belonged to my father. Listen and you will hear its pulse.' He dangled the pocket watch for Kalif to hear and see.

'Ah, let me have it,' gasped the grasshopper, gaping at the timepiece in wonderment.

'Catch it if you can!' challenged Marcel, throwing the watch to the insect. The boy then tugged at the bristle and slipped out in the wink of an eye while Kalif, who had snatched the watch in mid-air, was lovingly admiring the timepiece as the leaf closed over him.

Without giving a second glance back, Marcel hobbled on to the clearing, accompanied by the brief muffled cries of the grasshopper; then nothing more did the boy hear as he slumped to the ground.

17

The Lily Pond

The first light of morning is undisputedly the best time of day in the summer to pasture if you are a snail; any later would put you in peril of clomping feet, dipping beaks, and snooping muzzles. And indeed many of them were already snailing across the dewy lawn by the time the sun began to show over the eastern ridge, flooding the plain in a yolkish sheen. A croaky cockerel sounded the crack-of-dawn call, while an ammophila, which is a spindly two-winged insect with an orange waistband, shook a leg from its bizarre sleeping position. It slept clamped onto a grass stalk by the sheer force of its mandibles while holding out its hard chitinous body as stiff as a plank at right angles to the vertical. There were certainly some advantages to having your skeleton inside out.

A solitary mason bee, up with the first sunbeams, zoomed by and alighted on her snail-shell dwelling where she continued her toil of packing her offspring in snug self-contained apartments. And down by the lily pond, where the straggling veils of mist were being dissipated, there came a movement near the bulrushes. A male toad straddled out on the bank, carrying its clutch like a sack of glutinous berries on its back.

All this Marcel looked upon in wonder from inside a flower's crown. It had just opened, offering him the breathtaking spectacle of the start of day, as well as breakfast in bed.

At length he climbed down from his viewpoint and made his way to the edge of the bank to further admire the show. At that point it was raised thirty odd centimeters above the water line, which on Marcel's present terms made it no different from looking from the top of a cliff. Except, of course, that bulrushes and reeds do not usually tower over cliffs. He gave a sigh of contentment with the prospect of the new day and a whole life before him. Kalif had been right to be envious. As a young human born into a free society, he had the liberty to escape his condition, to take his destiny in his own hands, and to make something singular of his existence on earth with whatever potential he had. Anything else, he conceded, would be a waste of time, and talent to boot.

The neighboring ammophila gave itself a wash down then took off over the pond where dragonflies were already patrolling. The father toad had just dropped into the water to deliver the fruit of his labor into the element of creation. After a quick rub with hind legs, the eggs were released, and moments later tadpoles were hatching everywhere, while the toad was already sneaking away, only too glad to pick up the threads of his bachelor business.

But the beauty of the scene only enhanced the ugliness Marcel felt inside. For one, be it his fault or not, the bare truth was that he had abandoned his friends. Not as the toad had abandoned his offspring, leaving them to their own fate, for the valiant amphibian had delivered them to their natural element. He, Marcel, had taken his friends out of theirs and left them where they could have perished. And what made things worse, *they* had risked their lives to save *him*.

Then there was Henriette. To think he was so imbued with his own person that it did not even occur to him that she could have any qualms over the aspirations of her parents. Aspirations that not so long ago he was perfectly willing to go along with. At last he was seeing perhaps the ugliest part of his person: that part steeped in pride.

He was quite handsome, quite intelligent, quite talented, and he quite knew it. But what difference would all that make to Henriette, who wanted nothing more than love and someone to care for?

He recalled that scene in her bedroom when they were young kids. He had suggested they play prince and princess. She retorted that she would rather play mothers and fathers, asserting that given she had inherited her father's traits she had no illusions of becoming a princess. She only ever dreamt of marrying someone she could love, he remembered her saying, and that someone was evidently Wilfried. The place on earth Henriette prized most was that of a loving wife and mother, which Marcel now recognized as being as praiseworthy as his high-minded ambitions, if not more so. After all, without such likeminded women, how could humanity survive?

How he had evolved so callously in his cocoon of conceit. And now that it was unraveling, he felt uglier by the minute, ashamed of his behavior toward Henriette, ashamed of taking a shot at a shortcut to wealth. It was Julia's last words that ricocheted round his brain now: *Are you a profiteer, or a coward?* she had said.

He cast his eyes out again from his introspection over the pond. They fell upon a nymph clinging to a reed stem in the sun. The bulging thorax suddenly split open, and an adult dragonfly gradually and smartly slipped out of its nymphal suit grown too small. Its birth gave him a vent for his emotions. And looking off the cliff, he went and did something quite silly for someone so proud: he sat down on the ledge and cried.

***

'I'm sure they'll grow back, Marcel,' said Bea supportively while approaching him from behind. 'Look on the bright side, at least they shortened them both to the same-ish length, and honestly I think shorter antennas suit you better!'

Marcel quickly drew a cuff across his eyes and without turning said, 'Thanks, Bea, but it's not my antennas I feel rotten about; it's because I've been so...

self-centered…with Henriette, with Julia, and now with you lot. I left you all in the house; you could have gotten killed, and it would have been entirely my fault.'

'What do you mean?' said Bea, evidently quite slighted. 'Huh, getting out of houses is child's play; we weren't born with the last dewfall you know!'

'Especially when you've got a dedicated and un-wivalled guide amongst ya!' added Brim, joining them.

'Yes, thankfully a gallfly came and told us you'd gotten into bad company with a hoverfly, and hoverflies can be jolly deceitful, you know,' said the bee, not purposely snubbing the inchworm but snubbing him all the same.

'Hmm, I do now,' said Marcel.

'But it *was* yours twuly who got us back to the hall where we bumped into the gallfly,' said Brim, quick to underline his role in their escape.

Bea continued, 'She gave us the idea to hitch a ride on that hairy mop friend of yours.'

'Mop?' said Marcel, turning round with his shortened antennae standing straight on their ends, which was equal to a raised eyebrow.

'The mop with four legs!'

A smile pleated Marcel's mouth as he returned, 'You mean the dog!'

'Mop, dog, whatever, anyway it had been out twice already, so we figured it might go out again. We climbed on its rear quarters when it was asleep and waited.'

'Until at last it called the old marcelette, and we were out!' added Brim.

'Boggin' rotten ride, though,' said a glum voice from a hollow in the rockery. 'It went all over the boggin' place 'til it ended up at the pond, then it must have picked up your trail,' continued the rhino.

'If only we'd have gotten there for you sooner we'd have saved your carapace!' said the bee.

'My carapace?' questioned Marcel, getting to his feet, and with his eyes he followed Bea's sorrowful glance down to his lapels in shreds. 'Oh, you mean my jacket,' chuckled Marcel and explained that humans have their skeleton on the inside and that because of their soft skin, they wear extra artificial layers called clothing to protect it. To push home his explanation to the slightly perplexed insects, Marcel opened his jacket and undid his shirt collar. 'There,' he said, '*that* is human skin!'

'Looks more like chitin to me!'

'No, Rhino, skin is much softer, see?' insisted Marcel, patting the region between his collarbones and felt for a pinch of flesh. But the touch was not as he had remembered, and he could gather no heaps of skin between forefinger and thumb. Instead, looking down at his torso, he undid his buttons further, and the horrifying reality sunk in as he felt the hard smooth surface of his bare chest.

'God, it *is* chitin!' gasped the boy, looking up in horror.

'Hmmm, put it this way, if it weren't, you'd have every female mosquito in the neighborhood swarming around you by now, not for your looks, mind, for your blood,' said Rhino, hobbling into the daylight from the shade of his overnight quarters. Marcel realized in a flash that if Kalif's claws had left no wound on his leg, it was because of his new carapace. However, the dread of another metamorphosis was suddenly quashed as quickly as it had risen on seeing the sheenless beetle advance with a limp and only one antenna.

'Bloody hell, Rhino, you're injured!'

'No worry, Marcel.'

'But it's my fault!'

'No, it's just me getting a bit long in the horn. You become fragile when you get old.'

'Old?' said Marcel pulling a woeful face, as if his one-horned friend had contracted a terrible disease.

'Yup, ageritus, it's one of Ma Nature's little foibles in exchange for giving us a crack at life, else we'd all just go on and on and on 'til we got eaten.'

'But you can't get old yet, Rhino,' entreated Marcel. 'Look, don't worry, we'll get you to the royal jelly before it gets any worse; it can work wonders, can't it, Bea?'

'It can certainly make a queen out of a commoner.'

'No, Marcel, I'll never make it all the way round the pond to the tree,' said Rhino resignedly.

A bowel movement resounded from Brimstone's direction, and he said, 'I'm not so sure I will either, now you mention it, I can alweady feel the changes coming on!'

'And I can smell 'em!' said Rhino.

'Then we'll go over it!' declared Marcel with fresh fighting spirit for the new cause. But before he could say anymore, a female human voice sang out from a short distance.

'Henri-ette. Henriette, there you are,' it said on approaching. 'What are you looking at?'

'Oh, Julia, I was just listening to the pond waking. If you listen carefully, you can hear the chatter of insects. There must be a grasshopper down there, I could hear its little chirp.'

'I do believe you are in love, Henriette Deforge, and I must say it suits you!'

'Oh, but it's horrible,' said Henriette in a sudden sob of despair. The two cousins were standing just a few meters from Marcel, who could make out their giant figures through the undergrowth of bulrush stems that separated them from him. 'How am I going to tell mother and father about Wilfried?'

'Gosh, you really are such a snob!' said Julia, embracing her cousin.

'It's not my fault; it's the way I've been brought up,' said Henriette, dashing away the welling tears with her forefingers before they could stream down her cheeks.

'Never mind, lucky for you it can be cured. As long as you learn to assert your true self.'

'That's easy for you to say.'

'God, you're worse than Marcel. You only have to put your mind to it and open your mouth. Just tell them you're going out with him and that it's your choice. If you don't, you'll probably end up a spinster like aunt Lucille.'

'You're right, I know you are, but I can't,' said Henriette in desperation.

'You'll have to, otherwise, knowing Wilfried, you might never see him again; he's so stuck on his principles. Going by what you said he said yesterday, if the bees go, so will he. And need I remind you the beekeeper's supposed to be coming this evening. It's your last chance, Henriette. Either you want Wilfried and take him as he is, or you don't.'

'Now you put it like that... Oh, Julia, he might not be handsome, but I couldn't live without ever seeing him again. He makes me feel...loved. Do you understand?'

'No, but I hope to one day. Look, why don't you tell your mother first? I know what, after my appointment I'll bring up the subject then you take it from there.'

'Yes, all right, I will,' said Henriette, putting on a braver face. 'What do you think the solicitor wants this time by the way?'

'I've an awful feeling he's found another one of daddy's debts,' sighed Julia.

'Father always said he was a bit of an adventurer, though.'

'Is that what you think?'

'No. I always thought he was very clever, and I used to wish father could be as gentle.'

'He was a brilliant inventor. But it's true, inventions don't necessarily pay the bills, do they?'

'At least he had the courage of his convictions, didn't he?' said Henriette, who in her present predicament put courage higher than any other virtue.

'And left wife and child without a penny, that's the bare truth of it,' said Julia. 'And now thinking about it, I'm beginning to wish I hadn't lectured Marcel with daddy's conception of life, about trying to make a dream come true. After all, sometimes it just doesn't work out, people sometimes die beforehand. And some people just aren't cut out for it. That's probably why Marcel's disappeared.'

'Don't worry about Marcel. I expect he's gone to his aunt's,' said Henriette, who gave her cousin a kiss on the cheek.

'Mommy's afraid the solicitor declares us bankrupt this time. She couldn't face up to seeing him,' continued Julia in her matter-of-fact way. But Marcel wasn't duped, even without seeing her face square on, he detected in her voice that something had shaken her confidence at the very roots. Indeed, Julia had spent half the night preparing for losing her illusions with regards to her father's values and realizing that all he had left her with was an unstable childhood, a depressed mother, and a precarious future.

The girls suddenly turned their heads in unison on the sound of the rustle of a dress approaching.

'And I'm not so sure we'll be able to bail you out again,' said Madame Deforge sternly on overhearing the end of the conversation. 'Come along now, chop, chop, if we want to be at the solicitor's by nine. And then there's shopping to do for the party!'

As they parted, Marcel, with extra determination to prove to Julia the virtue of her father's convictions, turned to his friends, who had huddled around him. 'Come on! Let's fly down to that lily pad,' he said, pointing a finger over the cliff down to the lower level where the bank sloped gently into the water. This is where the curling lily pad in question sat deprived of its element by weeks of summer sun. 'Bea, can you take off yet?'

'No, I tried already, but I should think I can glide though.'

'I can't even do that. I'm jammed, remember?' groused Rhino in answer to which Marcel strode to the beetle businesslike and tugged at his wing casings. At last there was a click, and both the insect's wings were released and humming for liftoff.

'Last one to hit the lily pad's a stinkbug!' cried Marcel before spreading his own wings and gliding off the cliff after the rhinoceros into the bright and fresh morning air.

'Hey, that's not fair!' called Brim. He had no choice but to inch down the cliff face while Bea, too, dipped over the ledge and, for the first time since her meeting with Rhino, entered into flight.

There was no doubt that the winged marcel had made progress since his first flight, and he landed just short of the target with the bee managing to hold the horizon close behind. The rhinoceros however made quite a hash of it and landed stranded upside down, further up the shore where the winter waterline was delimited by the vegetation.

'Flap your wings, Rhino!' called out Marcel on seeing the beetle pawing the air.

'Boggin' bluebells, what do you think I'm trying to do? They're stuck!'

Marcel and Bea promptly rallied to lend the poor coleopteran a hand.

'I'm getting too old for all this palaver. There's no escaping the fact, time's catching up with me,' he said.

'Nonsense,' said the bee. taking position beside his flank. 'Just keep pushing with your wings. I don't want you on my conscience; I've enough to worry about.'

The boy and the bee heaved against the beetle's flank and soon had him back on his feet.

'There,' said Marcel with a tap on his horn. 'Liven up, my gran used to say, you're as old as you feel!'

'That's precisely the problem; I feel exactly as old as me chitin, which makes me one hundred and thirty two days old. And I'm afraid that puts me on the short list; it's Nature's way.'

'There's still life in you yet, Rhino. Just keep your mind on getting to the royal jelly. I'm sure Mother Nature won't bear a grudge against you for having a bit of extra easy living!' said the boy.

'I've been thinking about it, Marcel. See, that's not our way.'

'Well you don't think we've come this far just to leave you here to die, do you?'

'Why not?' asked Rhino, surprised.

'Because that's not my way, to live and let die is a crime in my world. When people get ill, we make them better. At least we try.'

'It don't work every time then?' said Rhino.

'Well no, actually, it didn't work on my dad,' admitted Marcel. 'He caught a disease. They did try very hard to heal him, though.'

The unexpected exposure of the painful memory made the boy's heart suddenly heavy with grief and guilt.

'You mean they didn't?' said Rhino gravely.

'Didn't they give him any royal jelly?' said Bea softly.

'No, Bea, they tried with other cures, but they couldn't stop the disease from spreading. If I'd been older, I don't know, maybe I could have done something, but they kept me out of the way. And to be honest, I wasn't that worried at first. They said he was going to be all right. But then he just kept getting worse, and the next minute, he was slipping through my fingers without me realizing, and I didn't get a chance to tell him things, or even lift a finger to help him. Then he died.'

The words carried with them packets of grief and guilt out of his body and were replaced by a kind of soothing feeling that gradually seeped into the space they had occupied all those years. Nevertheless, steering his mind from private matters back to the issue at hand, with an encouraging smile, he said, 'But don't worry, Rhino, it wasn't ageritus, and I'm older now, and we have a cure. So come on, there's no time to waste.'

Brimstone meantime, oblivious to all the chinwag, had arrived as cool as a cucumber on the lily pad, quite content with himself, and declared, 'Last one on the lily pad's a stinkbug!' And the rhino, the bee, and Marcel were soon racing back to the water's edge.

Marcel cut away the anchorage of the lily pad. Then, with the aid of Brim's chompers, he stripped a leaf of its veins, cut the remaining stalk to size, and threw it into the embarkation for use during the crossing.

The passengers prudently boarded the raft; Marcel gave a mighty push off and hopped in all in one go. And my word, if anyone had gone for a dawn stroll around the lily pond that fine morning, they would certainly have rubbed their eyes twice at the singular sight of a rhino, an inchworm, and a honeybee being paddled across the glazed-like surface by a marcel, of the winged variety.

***

The lily leaf raft slipped serenely over the water's surface under the thrust of Marcel's makeshift paddle amid whirligig beetles just beginning to stir. Only a few times did any ripples come to disturb the ambient tranquility—a plop from the bank here, a splosh from a lily leaf there—each time the crew turned their heads too late. Yet if their eyes were more knowing, they would have picked out the waking tree frogs squatting here and there, patiently awaiting their breakfast. That said, only once did any fright really stir aboard.

They were about to enter a sparsely reeded area where Marcel had spotted an ideal place to disembark without getting their feet wet when he stopped paddling and pointed up ahead.

'Yikes!' he let out under his breath. 'Don't move!' All eyes followed the lad's finger and picked out a newborn dragonfly sunning its unfurled wings on a reed, which happened to be in their trajectory. It was the same dragonfly that had given vent to his emotion on the ledge of the bank.

'If you ask me, I'd say its gonna be hungwy!' said Brim.

'Do you really think we ought to go on?' said Bea, looking timorously up at the satin-blue hunter par excellence.

'I don't see anywhere else we can moor up. We can hardly go back now, and we've got to get Rhino to the royal jelly. And besides that, the floor's letting in water,' said Marcel, lowering his glance to the middle of the raft floor where the leaf had been most dehydrated.

'Bah, it's probably not fit for flying yet; besides, whoever heard of a dragonfly zooming down on a lily pad for its breakfast?' said the veteran rhinoceros beetle.

'Twue, dwagonflies usually catch their bweakfast in midflight. But saying that, there are exceptions to evewy wule,' reflected the inchworm.

'That's true, hah. If anyone 'ad told me this time yesterday I'd be floating across a pond on a lily leaf with an inchworm and a honeybee, let alone a marcel, I'd 'a' told 'em to hop it!' said Rhino, whose deep chuckle did not reflect the general feeling of alarm.

'Shhh! It'll hear you!' said Miss Bea curtly.

Marcel gave another anxious glance at the bottom of the boat to see the puddle slowly widening.

'Looks like we've no other choice. Well they say that fortune favors the brave. We'll just have to keep a low profile and a vigilant eye out,' said the lad in the role of captain of the vessel.

So with tantalizing slowness, Marcel eased the raft discreetly round and between the reeds, while all else on board kept one eye on the dragonfly and another on the puddle growing in the middle. But, thankfully, the dragonfly did not budge, and at last they were moving up against the draping branch of a bush that jutted out as good as a jetty.

'Come on, your turn, Rhino, get your carcass up there!' said Marcel after the inchworm had hoisted himself up onto the overhanging leaf from the lily pad.

Not without some more remonstrance, the rhino was soon heaved onto the leaf face then hobbled behind the inchworm along the branch toward the dry bank where a myriad of flowers colored their view. Bea followed, with Marcel keeping up the rear.

'Mmm, I say, smells like home,' buzzed the bee, taking in the different essences of the flower garden that separated them from the lime tree where the honeybees had set up home. On the realization that his quest must soon come to an end, Marcel felt his chest sink a moment into melancholy, which—to look on the bright side—at least suggested his heart was still human. Deep down, though, he was quite looking forward to the ultimate metamorphosis, that of a boy into a young man with a firm resolution in life, provided he got to the royal jelly in time.

New and delicious fragrances filled his antennae as he continued over the woody jetty with the pond glistening below. It suddenly occurred to him that he ought at least find out what a winged-marcel looked like. This certainly meant a daunting face-to-face, but curiosity got the better of him. He got down on all fours, braced himself, and taking a good grip, leaned over the edge of the branch to discover, by and by, the reflection of his chitin, which gave him a nice smooth green complexion, and his shortened antennae, which were nonetheless smarter than he had imagined and definitely gave him a more commanding air. But the most magical sight of all was when he leaned over further, half turning his shoulders, to appreciate his lattice-veined wings. A little short, perhaps, but no less chic.

'Marcel, watch it; you might fall in,' called the irrevocable guide up ahead. But sure of his gripping powers, Marcel leant over a little more to fully admire his wings. It was then he was struck by a horrifying notion. 'Bloody hell, I'm not turning into a grasshopper am I?' he said to himself, and he instantly pictured a version of himself as the conceited, vile, and treacherous Kalif he most certainly did not want to resemble.

'Marcel, be careful else you'll fa...' called Bea, but she had not finished her sentence when a green blur sprang up from goodness knows where and gobbled the winged marcel down in one go!

The trio stood gaping, incapable of speech, at the space that a second earlier Marcel had occupied and then at the lily raft where the frog had landed. Until at last they managed to shriek their horror in unison, 'Buarrrghhhhhh!' To which the frog bulged out its gullet and returned a belly burp; Marcel shot back out of the batrachian's mouth like a human canon ball. In his surprise at being gobbled up and then double surprise at finding himself shooting through the air, the thought occurred to him too late to spread his wings to prolong his flight to the bank. Instead he shot like bolt headfirst into the water. He did, however, think to use them once under water to give himself extra propulsion, and at length he hauled himself up the bank, heavy with water clinging to limbs and sticking to wings.

Seconds after collapsing on the damp shore, he closed his eyes to the voice of Bea saying, 'And thank goodness frogs don't like marcels!'

18
Ma Nature's Light

'Look at them; they're in tatters,' deplored Marcel, twisting his torso to glimpse at his wings. He was sitting on a sunny pebble where a short time earlier his friends had dragged him to dry out. Bea was finishing off fan drying him with her wings.

'They're not meant for flying underwater, you know,' she said above the buzz.

'At least the west of you is still in one piece, though!' Brimstone pointed out.

'Well, that's true, mustn't grumble s'pose. Thanks for pulling me out of the wet, anyway.'

'You can thank Whino's horn for that!' said Brimstone. During the ensuing silence, Marcel caught Bea give the inchworm a curt look. The boy scanned the immediate vicinity from the pond, not half a meter to his right, to the fringe of undergrowth that led into the flower garden to his left.

'Where is Rhino anyway?' he said, sensing something was up as the bee stopped fanning.

'Um, well, he wandered off actually, while you were still flat out on the stone,' she harrumphed at last. 'He said he wanted to be alone.'

'It's because his time is up, Marcel,' said Brim in all honesty.

'It is nature's way,' said Bea.

Marcel promptly slid off the pebble and furiously demanded, 'Which way did he go?' Bea pointed toward a gap in the vegetation. 'Come on!' he said. But no sooner had he taken a step forward than a loud vibrant monotone music filled the air around the little alcove and arrested his movement. Seconds later his suspicions were confirmed when Kalif's dastardly lieutenants burst out from the thicket, dragging the rhinoceros by the horn behind them on his back, followed by none other than Kalif in person!

'No, Marcel, this is not another nightmare, or if it is, you won't be waking from it!' snarled the chief grasshopper, now standing on his hind legs in front of the beetle.

'Kalif,' returned Marcel, 'I thought I left you feeding your favorite plant!'

'Ha, if you keep perfectly still, the plant does not crush, it does not release its digestive substances, and it opens its pretty leaf again,' returned Kalif, lordly conceding his knowledge while at the same time barely containing his scathing temper. 'But now I've a score to settle with you. Not only is your timepiece of no living fiber, but also you've wasted my precious time. Now you will pay!'

Kalif's eyes, though murderous, in the broad daylight peered with but a glimmer compared to their intense glare of the night before. And Marcel, invested with new confidence in his suit of chitin, this time stood unflinchingly before him.

'What do you want?'

'You. Unless you'd rather us share the last meal of this old carcass here!' wheezed Kalif sardonically, while his henchmen grinned hungrily over the beetle's gut. 'It *was* a surprise bumping into him on our way here.'

'Get away, Marcel. Save yourselves; my time's up anyway!' croaked Rhino. With the flick of a claw, Kalif gave the order to sever the beetle's remaining antenna. Marcel's blood was now blazing with fury. The boy glared full into Kalif's gaze and held it with defiance while reaching for his knife, which a second later went wheeling through the air. It felt like a good direct hit the instant it left his hand. Indeed it sank with a thud right between Kalif's eyes, leaving the grasshopper to pause introspectively a moment before, boss-eyed, he keeled over.

Marcel swiftly followed up with a great bound, and even before the chief grasshopper had hit the ground, the boy was coursing down feet first upon the first lieutenant in a fabulous flying-kick that left the creature lying sprawled out and inert over the ground with a dislocated head, while the second lieutenant plain upped and hopped it.

'See you need no looking after now,' said Rhino with a faint chuckle in his gullet as Marcel, Bea, and Brimstone rallied to his side to heave him back over.

'Oof, waf, waf, oiya!' he croaked on landing upright to find the world back under his feet.

'Try not to waste your energy, Rhino. Just eat some pollen,' said Marcel, while Bea passed some over.

'Bah, no use. Take no offence, Miss Bea.'

'None taken, Master Rhino,' said the bee, who understood the score, as did Brim, who bowed his head dolefully.

'Come on, chin up, Rhino, not far to the royal jelly now,' said Marcel, trying to put on a brave face, though deep down sensing that this time his friend would not be going any further.

'My time has come, Marcel, and that's all there is to it. And it's nobody's fault.'

'Yes, it is,' lamented the boy. 'If I hadn't provoked your collision with Bea, if I hadn't looked into the pond...'

'Na, stop your griping and listen up while there's still a breath in me.' Here the beetle paused a moment and looked squarely at them all standing in front of him about as merry as a mole hole. With one stub of an antenna shorter than the other, he indeed looked in poor shape. He resumed. 'Truth is, I was on my last legs anyway, and my wings were already worn out when I bumped into Miss Bea, and I don't regret it a bit either. See, I've always been a loner, used to sneer at social gatherings of insects huddling together, though I admit many a time I wondered what it must be like to be in with the crowd. Since we met, you've shown me that and taught me the warmth of friendship, and, well, I might not look like it lying 'ere like this, but I'm mighty grateful for the lesson.'

To this Bea sobbed. 'So am I glad we bumped into each other.'

'If it weren't for you, Master Whino, and all your great force we wouldn't have got this far!' said Brimstone.

'Pick your chin up off the floor, Inchworm! And no point blubberin', dame, and you needn't pull such an ugly face, either, Marcel,' said Rhino with spirit, despite his waning voice. Then slowly nodding his great head with sagacity, he said, 'See, we go through life from one metamorphosis to the next, from conception to birth, to infancy, to youth, to adulthood, through to old age. They are the rites of passage we all must face up to; they allow us to reach our true destiny, and remember…' The rhino paused a slow second to catch Marcel's eye. 'I've a feeling maybe your dad didn't get time to tell you, but you must neither be sad nor afraid to pass through them, Marcel. Now you are to move into youth, a time for new tastes and budding passions. Be careful in choosing which ones to cultivate! As for me, I have passed through them all, so my journey in this world ends. But think of my departure as the ultimate metamorphosis; I'm no longer sad nor afraid, so you needn't be neither. After all, I'm off through Ma Nature's light to paradise. Now fair wind to you all…and remember, don't be afraid.' Rhino concluded in a last baritone whisper, and he softly laid down his great head peacefully on the ground.

'Rhino?' said the lad after a respectful silence and gently tugged the insect's horn. But the beetle's fixed gaze had already lost its glimmer.

'He's gone, Marcel. He's gone through the tunnel to Ma Nature's light,' said Bea, looking toward the sky. 'Come, we'd better be moving on.'

***

But a short time later found the three companions still at the same spot, sitting half exhausted beside a hump of soft earth.

'You can tell it to me a hundwed times over, Marcel, I still can't see the point of buwying Whino's body,' said the inchworm, chewing on some pollen. 'Someone might have got some extwa use out of it, be it just as an energizer!'

'Yes, even Rhino would have bawled at us for wasting time,' said Bea.

'Let's just say it's the way we do things where I come from; besides, it's done now,' said Marcel.

'Well I bet he's looking down on us having a wight ole gripe.'

19
The Flower Garden

The inchworm led the way through the flower garden. It ran along the driveway some half a dozen meters all the way to the shade of the great lime tree whose massive branches spread out a thousand meters above their heads, at least so it seemed to Marcel. The sun was soon shining down at a pretty steep angle, and flowers unblushingly offered their fullest bloom in anticipation of another great day's pollinating.

The colorful flowerscape and rush of perfumes little by little lifted Marcel's spirits. And with the growing warmth, insects of every hue and nature resumed their 'buzziness.' Was it the influence of the spectacular surroundings or did Marcel detect a note of merriment in the ambient buzz? At any rate, every insect he passed by stood before him with respect and congratulated him on his heroic feat. Indeed, killing Kalif was all over the garden, and ants had already dissected his body into a hundred morsels. The tyrannical grasshopper who had challenged Mother Nature's spirit was thus woven back into the fabric of her design. And even the grasshoppers were glad to be able to get back to the normal condition of insect life.

'We'll stop here and take some refreshment,' said Marcel at length then shinned up a stalk to get a clear view over the canopy of flowers. Turning his head, he was nearly knocked off balance as his retinas were smacked by the sheer force of the magnificent lime tree. Its great trunk rose up like a striated mountain face barely a dozen meters before him. 'Wow, that's your tree, is it, Bea?' he said, pointing to the colossus.

'I must hold my tongue to that question,' said the bee, buzzing up and hovering happily beside him now that she had regained the full use of her wings. 'But I can say it is awfully good to be nearly home again,' she added as a strong hint.

'And a stately home it is, too. Look wight up there, Marcel,' said Brim, looping his head upward. 'There's your woyal jelly, mate! Only snag is getting up there!'

Marcel followed Brimstone's turn of head and picked out a hollow three meters up the trunk. Judging by the number of what he took to be bees congregating around it, at last he had found the nest that would bear him back to humanity. But from his present perspective, it was as good as being halfway up Mont Blanc.

The three companions had tracked over three quarters of the way across the garden, only stopping at brief intervals for a quick dip into low-lying or draping flowers within their reach. The sun was approaching midday; it was high time for rest and refreshment, and with every degree of sweetness under the sun, there was no place finer for both discerning palate and gulping gourmand. Indeed it was a struggle to choose which flower to dip into next, let alone where to stop and lounge. And, consequently, Marcel hopped from flower to flower in a bout of nectar tasting, enjoyed under the guidance of nectarologist, Miss Bea. At last, feeling plumb full up, he settled on some soft clover in a slightly tipsy daze. Bea, who had incidentally been uncharacteristically frugal in her takings, buzzed alongside him and said, 'I say, Marcel, it's such a relief to recover the full use of ones wings. Now while you're having a rest, I thought I'd just buzz off for a test flight. Shan't be long.' And as an afterthought, she added, 'And remember what I told you: don't go overindulging.'

The bee bumbled off, leaving Marcel feeling quite at peace with the world, despite his own tattered wings having fallen off, as he nestled into the cushion of clover. But after a short time, his rest was interrupted by a couple of seven-spotted ladybirds.

'Why don't you try resting in this one, Master Marcel? It's softer, and you'll be safer off the ground,' said one of them smiling shyly at the Kalif-killer from the stem of a thornless rose.

'We've cleared it of greenflies for you; it's perfectly spick and span, and the nectar is done just right!' assured the other, equally glad to be of service to the new 'lord' of the land. Marcel was happy to take up their offer and was soon climbing between the cool and silky-soft petals of the rose flower. The ladybirds had just taken their leave, undoubtedly eager to tell of their encounter with the intrepid marcel, when Brim called out to him.

'Looks like you've got admiwers, Marcel,' he said, lumping his body over the brim of the flower. Marcel was about to answer when his eyes fell upon a sight to remember. A beautifully colored butterfly, whose fine wings dazzled in the sunlight, was unfurling her trunk into a nectary of a purple buddleia flower nearby. Marcel motioned to the inchworm now clambering into the flower pit.

'Cor, ain't she a beauty! You don't often see one of those awound these parts,' said Brim moments later when he got a clearer view.

'What makes you think it's a she?' questioned Marcel in an equally low voice as the butterfly took to the wing.

'The colors for one; he-butterflies are wicher, to turn the eye of the faiwer sex.'

At that moment Marcel caught a glimpse of another butterfly that settled in the shade of the nearby overhanging willow. This one though was pretty much of a plain Jane compared to the flamboyant hues of the first. Again Marcel drew the inchworm's attention.

'Another butterfly to the left...hah, don't fancy yours much, Brim!'

'For your information, that's a moth,' humphed the inchworm. 'Butterflies close their wings when they land, their scales are smaller, and they have trunks!' he said and added quite dejectedly, 'And for your extwa information, that is what I'm s'posed to turn out like if we don't do something about it. I ask you, you can hardly say she sticks out in the cwowd! You wouldn't know she was there unless you bumped into her.' But his plaintive plea soon gave way to plain glee on looping his head toward the beautiful African monarch butterfly that had settled again at the same perfumed flower cluster as before. 'She weally is a beauty. If only...' he sighed, completely besotted and then, leaning over the flower toward the butterfly on the buddleia bush, he said in his most charming voice, 'Good morning, Miss. I say, I've warely seen such glowious livewy.'

'Rarely? How frightful! You mean I've competition around these parts?' said the butterfly.

'Oh, no, no, just a manner of speech. I meant, never. I've *never* ever seen such glowious livewy!' said the inchworm, literally bending over backward in an effort to repair his gaucherie.

'That's all right then. Though, you can hardly say the competition is rife in these parts, can you?' said the butterfly, fleetingly turning to the plain yellow moth in the willow.

'Competition or no competition, I would look at you all day long,' declared the inchworm gallantly.

'It must be disconcerting for the duller orders, but one mustn't blow ones own trumpet though, must one?'

'Oh, no, no,' said the inchworm, lapping up every word of the beautiful butterfly who sat pretty pleased to find such a cooperative and gullible admirer.

'Your own coloring's quite...something, too. If you've got it, flaunt it; that's what I say!'

'Oh, yes, that's exactly what I say, too, birds of a feather, eh.'

'When are you changing into your courting suit, by the way?'

'Oh, not long now at all, only four hundwed and twelve paces to go, you know.'

'Very interesting!'

'And do you know,' continued Brimstone passionately, 'I'm very strong, too. Yes, I took on a score of gwasshoppers and singled-tailed, knocked 'em stupid. Whack, whack, whack, I went!' he said, flexing his tail with every *whack* to give extra body to his narration.

As the inchworm related his fantastic adventures (made even more fantastic by adding zeroes to enemy head-counts), Marcel made a straw out of a stamen and supped up another mouthful of nectar before nestling drowsily between the perfumed petals of his host flower.

And in the blithe company of his companion and the beautiful butterfly, the boy slipped into the notion that maybe at last he had found a place to set down roots where he could feel he belonged, a place where he could start over with all the force of Mother Nature and the intelligence of man. Here he had everything, here everyone now knew him, here he was respected. Maybe he could help insects lead a better life. He could definitely forge a comfortable place for himself in a world like this. Now that he had sussed it, now with his new powers, he could come to govern it even. He lay there parading through his mind all the things he could do if he became an insect emperor.

'But you don't belong here,' said a warm baritone voice. Marcel raised his heavy-lidded eyes and standing before him as large as life was the rhino. The boy looked contemplatively an instant down at the nectar he had tapped into and back again at Rhino, or was it a figment of his imagination? But the figment spoke again.

'Should you stay or should you go, Marcel?'

'Rhino! I thought you were dead and buried.'

'I am, at least my body is, thanks to you. You're speaking to my spirit. Now, to help you answer the question: is this truly your world, Marcel, here among us insects?'

'No, but I can adapt, and I'm settling in fine already.'

'But all this won't last: the flowers will wither, your fervor will fade, and it will be too late to pick up the path to your true destiny. Remember your resolution, have you so easily forgotten that? And your plan?'

'But I can have a new plan, be useful to this world.'

'No, you will always be a foreigner here. Deep down in your heart, no matter how hard you try, no matter what you do, no matter what you become, you will remain the essence of the being Mother Nature molded you as. This will be your condition throughout your life, even though you may pretend otherwise. It is that person you must discover—the real you—it is with that person you must find your own path, Marcel. To take someone else's is to betray that person deep inside of you.'

'But look at me, Rhino. You've got to admit, I'm as good an insect as any, and I still haven't gone through complete metamorphosis yet.'

'It is up to you, but answer this: why did you bury my bodily remains?'

'Well,' said Marcel, stumped for words, and the recollection of those said at the rhino's burial made their way to his memory: *Let's just say it's the way we do things where I come from,* was what the boy had said. 'I s'pose I buried you because I'm human,' he admitted, at last looking up, but the rhino was no longer there. Instead, when he raised his head, he saw the inchworm waddling where he had left him, trying to sweet-talk the stunning African monarch butterfly sunning her wings in the buddleia bush. If not quite seduced, she was certainly having fun with the attention.

'I'm not the marcel's second for nothing, you know...' Brimstone was saying, then quite sure of himself, he smoochily declared, 'So, I shall soon be available for courtship. And if you're still awound, I'd be honored if we could get together.'

'I say, you are a funny creature, I'll give you that,' laughed the butterfly. 'But there's no use getting ideas; you're not my type at all,' she replied categorically. 'Why don't you speak to the *moth* over there!' she continued, which certainly put a damper on Brim's hopes.

Meanwhile there came a rustle and a flap from the willow, and the moth in question said, 'A moth and proud to be one!' Then stepping out into the open, she said, 'And what does anyone want to look like a flower for anyway?'

'Because flowers are beautiful, darling,' said the African monarch butterfly.

'Flowers attract birds!'

'There's nothing wrong with birds, not when you've spent your whole caterpillarhood on a diet of milkweed as I have. Not everyone's cup of nectar, I grant you, darling, but it's the price for being able to flaunt ones beauty far and wide. No bird will even think of touching me, not unless they want poisoning!'

'Ah, so that's the secwet!' said Brim in a sigh of revelation.

'Huh, no secret to me,' said the moth. 'I ate some milkweed once by mistake, disgusting stuff! Brrr, give me fresh hawthorn any day, and you can keep your fancy looks.'

'Acquiring beauty is an art, darling. It's all a question of taste!' retorted the proud butterfly.

Before the moth could answer back, there came a loud buzz that made her dart back into the shade of the willow.

'Huh, run and hide, darling!' mocked the beautiful butterfly, sniggering frivolously.

'There's no need to be afraid. It's only Bea,' called Marcel.

Then while inching back into the open the moth said, 'Oh, yes, silly me, I get a bit on edge at this time of day. It's about this time that the birds get peckish, you know.'

Meanwhile Bea, who had landed awkwardly, was busy removing her snout from between the petals of the flower where Marcel, dipping another finger of nectar into his mouth, was looking quite emperor-ish.

'Mar-cel! There you are, I was worried you'd gotten eaten!' she said, now looking none too pleased to find him safe and cozy and visibly drunk on nectar.

'Hah, no chance. Marcel's a Kalif-killer, wemeber? He's the lord of the land wound 'ere now!' cheered Brimstone to Bea's further annoyance.

'And cute with it,' tittered the beautiful butterfly.

'Don't you think you've had enough? Mixing nectars is bad for you,' said Bea scoldingly then upbraided the inchworm, who ought to know better.

'Come on, take it easy, Bea,' said Marcel, lazily dipping another finger of nectar into his mouth.

'Yeah, just look awound you; this is the land of plenty!' added Brim.

'And hark who's raving on about mixing pollen,' piped in the beautiful butterfly. 'I saw you earlier with the marcel, and you didn't have sunflower pollen all over you then!' she remarked with a taint of irony.

'And since when do butterflies interfere with bee business?' asked Bea, looking levelly at the butterfly. Then to Marcel she said, 'Listen, Marcel, I'm going off to see the queen to arrange an audience for you. So you make your way to the foot of the tree.'

'But Bea, I'm not so sure I want to go back—'

'Nonsense, Marcel. Besides, you have to free Henriette. Now go to the foot of the tree, the beekeeper will be here soon, or have you forgotten?' she said, preparing for flight. Then, extracting a tiny flake of wax from between her abdominal segments, she added, 'Plus you've got to make up with Julia, or have you forgotten that, too? Here, I kept a little perfume just in case.' And she dropped a gorgeous smelling wax flake into his lap as she took to the air and buzzed up, up, and away toward the hollow in the lime tree.

'But Bea,' Marcel called after her, still wondering if he should stay or go.

The inchworm, meanwhile, had resumed the conversation where it left off before Miss Bea had come bumbling in. Still thoroughly bewitched by the butterfly's livery, he was saying, 'I'd personally eat anything to be able to flaunt my colors fweely like your good self.'

'Colors, darling? Are you forgetting you are one of hers,' said the beautiful butterfly, looping her head to her yellowish counterpart. 'If anything, you might get a tinge or two but nothing you'd want to go showing off.'

But the inchworm would not have any of it. 'I can change,' he said. 'I'm as good as any monarch caterpillar. Look, I can crawl like one. I'm just missing a splash of color, that's all, and the marcel's gonna help me get some royal jelly for that.'

'Why don't you stop kidding yourself and just accept who you are?' said the moth.

'I know who I am, and who I want to be, thanks!'

'Who are you then?' the moth questioned.

'Got pollen dust in your eyes? I'm a, I'm a...well can't you see who I am? I mean, isn't it obvious?'

'To be honest, Brim, right now you look like an inchworm trying to impersonate an African monarch caterpillar, but an inchworm all the same,' said Marcel, now more sober. Brimstone's claim had suddenly made the boy realize the absurdity of his own.

'But I *am* as good as any monarch caterpillar!' insisted Brimstone miserably.

'Then why are you afraid of birds?' said the beautiful butterfly. And, speaking of the devil, one swooped down.

'Cover!' shrieked the moth and flattened her body on a yellowing leaf of the willow, while Marcel and Brimstone dived between the petals of their flower.

As for the beautiful butterfly, she remained nonchalantly parading her gorgeous self on the buddleia cluster.

'Watch out!' called the moth, whose camouflage blended perfectly into the vegetation. 'Another bird above, this time a youngen!'

Instead of heeding the warning, the beautiful butterfly defiantly took to the sky in a magnificent flutter.

'Huh, you run and hide, darlings, don't fret over me, I—' But she did not get time to finish her sentence before the bird snapped her up, and she was gone!

At length, the moth folded back her wings, the marcel raised his eyes to see the sky all clear, and a flummoxed Brim gazed at the space where the beautiful butterfly had displayed her colors for the last time. Then he humbly said, 'I'm scared of birds because I'm an inchworm, I s'pose.'

'I thought she said she was poisonous to birds?' said Marcel, propping himself back up.

'African monarchs are, normally. It's just a pity that fledgling didn't know it, too. I expect it'll have learnt its lesson by tonight, though,' said the moth.

Just then, the sound of feet on gravel approached, and the moth took to the air. 'That's me off; birds won't come near while there's humans about,' she said, and off she fluttered farther afield.

'Weren't she just amazing?' said Brim, following her with his eyes.

'I thought you said you didn't fancy her,' said an amused Marcel.

'Oh, that was the old me talking. Now I've changed,' said Brim, still dreamily glancing at the departing brimstone moth with an affectionate glint in his eye. But his dream was soon broken as the voice of Monsieur Deforge suddenly resounded above the ambient buzz.

'Good of you to volunteer for service in the absence of Monsieur Cazeneuve, I must say.'

'He's been called out to another giant hornet nest,' said the unmistakable voice of Wilfried Delpech.

'Yes, I heard they're infesting the region.'

'They say they came aboard a ship from the Orient.'

'Anyway, you sure you'll be all right?'

'Yes, Monsieur Deforge. Sir, actually I've been assisting Monsieur Cazeneuve for the past year now, and I've jotted down the exact procedure here in my little book.'

'Good. Anyway, it's just as well you've showed up early with the women off shopping—save another scene, eh?'

'I hope you don't mind me asking, but has Henriette said anything about me?' ventured Wilfried, nervously straightening his glasses.

'No, not a word. Why, should she have?'

'Well, actually, there was something I wanted to talk to you about, sir.'

'Hmmm, oh, yes, hang on, now I think about it, she did say something about forgetting to pay your last lesson. Silly girl, wonder where she's got her head sometimes? She doesn't realize how well off she is compared to the lower orders, still—'

'No, no, er, it's not that,' said Wilfried. Struggling to get the words out, he gave an inadvertent glance up at the bee nest, which Deforge followed.

'Oh, don't worry about the bee nest. I'm sure she won't hold it against you.'

'No, no, of course. Well, I better get on. I have to get back to prepare my things for seminary college. I'm taking the early morning train. But will you please tell Miss Henriette I regret not being able to continue our piano lessons?'

'You needn't think any more of it. You get on with your life, dear boy; she'll understand. We'll soon find her another teacher.'

'Yes, of course,' said Wilfried, whose voice resounded with utter grief and deception.

'Right, while you're preparing for action, I'll fetch the long ladder,' said Deforge colonel-like and moved away toward the pigeon house.

'Flippin' heck! Quick, Brimstone, to the tree!' blurted Marcel, shaking off all lethargy and indecision, and they both tumbled out of the flower and scrambled headfirst down the stem.

20
The Apprentice Beekeeper

Across the open savannah of the parched but shaded driveway, they shifted toward the trunk of the great lime tree that stood planted like a mountain before them. Gleaming sunshine here and there dappled the ground below its boughs where some of its odorous blossoms had fallen in drifts, making it increasingly difficult to cut a straight path. The inchworm suddenly changed course to Marcel's surprise. 'Twust me!' said Brim. The boy was soon glad he did, as they shortly met with a protruding root that gave them a clear pathway the rest of the way to the tree trunk.

They had just reached the bark when a horrendous clamor clashed like thunder above their heads and boomed down through the exposed timber root they were travelling along. Marcel looked up to see Wilfried in his beekeeper's outfit setting the ladder against the tree. He then proceeded methodically in lengthening it so that it reached the branch nearest the hollow where the bee colony had set up home.

'Come on, Marcel, what are you waiting for? Up you go!' hollered Brim, seeing the boy check his step before the perilous vertical ascent. Marcel lacked neither confidence in his gripping power nor courage to ascend the furrowed tree face. But he knew full well that unless Wilfried went A over T, he would never make it to the nest in time.

'If only I could fly, I might stand a chance,' he blurted between breaths, 'but...one giant step to a hundred of mine, what's the point?' he said, shrugging his shoulders toward the giant in question.

'Don't give up now. You never know your luck; he might twip and bweak his neck!' remarked Brim, trying to be positive. Marcel glanced at the inchworm reproachfully then back again up at the ungainly giant, glasses steaming in his protective gear, as he approached the first rung barely two meters from where Marcel stood gawking almost in hope. But the very instant the wicked notion played on the boy's mind, it was chased away by the sound of a familiar drone.

'Hurry up and jump on my back; the queen's expecting you!'

'Bea! Good on you,' cheered Marcel above the buzz, while a couple of meters behind her, as luck would have it, Wilfried stopped in midstep, held out the smoker, which he had thankfully forgotten to light, and backstepped to his accessory box. 'But what about Brim?' said Marcel, turning back round to his companion.

'You forget about me, just you get going!'

'But—'

'Look, I've just one hundwed and eighty-two st-wides left in me before the changes start. It's time I found myself a nice bush where I can wwap up in!'

'But what about your colors?'

'Actually, I'd rather be without.'

'You're just saying that.'

'No, Marcel, I mean it. Hah, just think of the fun I shall have camouflaged on a tree.' Bwim grinned.

'Jump on, Marcel,' said Bea. The lad swung a leg behind her wings.

'Well, thanks, Brim, thanks for being my faithful guide,' he called out as she got her motor going.

'Thank *you* for helping me see my true colors! I shall be the pwoudest moth to bear bwown tinges who ever settled on a blackthorn twee,' hollered Brimstone, giving a gracious bow. Miss Bea worked up her wings to take-off velocity, as the smell of smoke wafted in their direction. The apprentice beekeeper was approaching the ladder again, this time with his tin smoker fuming at its beak.

'Hold on tight—up, up, and away,' Bea sang out and sprang into the air from the crest of the protruding root. But the very next moment found her plummeting like an oak apple to the ground, and she crash-landed with her passenger on a cushion of withering lime blossom. Marcel picked himself up first and promptly helped up the bee, none the worse for wear, to prepare for another take off. But her drooping antennae soon put him in the picture.

'Come on, Bea, you can't let me down now, not now that I've got everything sorted,' implored the boy.

'You're too heavy, Marcel. I did tell you not to overindulge.'

'Well, you'll just have to bring some royal jelly back to me here then, eh?'

'I can't; workers are the only ones allowed to feed it to the brood and the queen,' said Bea regretfully.

Marcel held his shortened antennae in the realization that he only had himself to blame. If only he had not lingered in the flower garden, he would not be helplessly watching Wilfried now placing one foot on the ladder to a life of remorse, neither would he himself be about to be deprived of living the only life he now knew he was cut out for. Instead he was going to turn into a bug for life.

Thoughts of ruining his future plans and the wasted love he had stored up for Julia suddenly invaded his entire being. Not to mention thoughts of the loneliness his failure would cause Henriette now that her lover had locked himself in an absurd now-or-never pact instead of taking the initiative of speaking out. If only the lanky scout would fall and break a leg, it would jolly well serve him right.

Marcel was seeing through the foolishness of man's pride all right, and consequently seeing his own. And although too late, he was becoming conscious, too, of the risk of man's fickle fancies. All these feelings whirled round in his gut in a maelstrom of remorse and despair. How could he have failed when Nature had given him every chance to succeed? If only he had heeded the voice

of his conscience, if only he had kept to his goal instead
of lingering.

In the midst of his introspection, he did not see
the little creature alight on the timber root that flanked
him and could only return a look of annoyance at Bea's
bizarre grin.

'Hu-hum, I hope you've still got some of your will
left, Marcel,' said a trill voice. In a split second, the boy
went from utter despair to almost celestial hope. Swallow and nod was all he could do until the wave of emotion passed.

'Good, because I think it might come in handy.
I've a message from the oak tree. Says you may be at one
with your conscience, but you still need to find your way
to the royal jelly.'

Marcel stood there an instant waiting in a kind of
bubble of expectation until, regaining command of his
emotions, at last he said, 'That it?' Then he questioned,
'But how can I?' And now feeling perfectly cheated, he
blurted, 'Wilfried will have smoked the nest out before
I even get halfway up the tree!'

'Why don't you just use your will?' said the gallfly
brightly. 'You did say it can lead you to great achievements.'

'It can, Gallfly,' said the boy, getting steadily into
a flap as a little yonder Wilfried proceeded cautiously
further up the ladder. 'But you still need to be in a position to use it. Bea can't carry me up there, and I'd be
surprised if you can.'

'No, I couldn't do that, Marcel. And besides, I was told you wanted to spread your *own* wings anyway.'

'Well I would if I could!' affirmed Marcel quite angrily while hunching up his shoulders to indicate that his wings had clean fallen off from his flying apparatus. But scarcely had he hammered out the last syllable than he was suddenly seized by spasms, made to fall to his knees while curving his head over his thorax and, for the second time in his strange adventure, two pairs of wings shot out of his back then swiftly unfurled and stiffened.

'Now, why don't you try?' said the gallfly when Marcel was done, as if metamorphosing were the most natural thing in the world.

After rising to his feet, he instinctively flapped his wings and found himself hovering effortlessly a few millimeters off the ground. Their span was such that they entered his field of vision with each downward stroke.

'They're beautiful, Marcel!' said Brimstone, who had crawled down the woody root to see the spectacle.

'A bit large perhaps,' remarked Miss Bea.

'They are full wings. Now fly, Marcel. There's no time to lose!' trilled the little gallfly before zooming away herself.

The large-winged marcel swiftly took to the air behind the honeybee. He swooped down and gave a last wave to Brimstone who doubled over backward in wonderment as the boy rose gracefully up into the sun-speckled foliage.

21

Chaos in the Nest

The ascent got Marcel's adrenaline flowing more sweetly than honey. Round and up he meandered behind Bea among a multitude of winged insects, some just pottering, others busy tucking into the pendant clusters of scented blossom. Fearing birds, the bee chose to lead the way under the cover of the dense foliage. Very soon Marcel was settling safely beside her a few steps from the entrance of the nest where bees were flying in and out. The strong smell of honey tinged with lime flower wafted over his antennae more deliciously than anything he could remember. And yet, now that he had arrived before the dimly lit vault of the hollow, an uneasy quiver sent a strange kind of foreboding to the pit of his belly. On top of this, a clomping sound from behind gave him a terrible scare. Quickly checking his back, his eyes fell on Wilfried, barely half a meter away, rearing his big veiled head over the bough the ladder was leaning against.

'Better get it done quick,' Marcel said.

'First, you must put this on,' said Bea and proceeded to douse the boy's antennae in a waxy secretion, while adding in a grave tone, 'Just keep your head down and follow my lead, and for goodness sake don't speak, even if spoken to. No one must find out you're a foreigner before we get to the queen.'

'Or what?' asked Marcel with a tremor in his throat as three more bees touched down on the bark then flew through the elongated hole in the tree trunk.

'At best, I suppose they'll throw you out.'

'And at worst?'

'Well, they could bite off your wings or sting you to death beforehand. But don't worry, come on,' said Bea about to enter.

'Hang on, I thought you got me an audience.'

'I did, but as the queen doesn't know you from Adam, and she doesn't know your scent, she can't trigger a friend pheromone for you. Come on; it'll be all right,' she said, leaving the boy nonetheless dubious as to whether he should set foot into the nest after all. But follow her he must if he was to grow up and claim the promise of his youth.

A voice called out from the foot of the tree. 'You sure you can handle it up there?' It belonged to Monsieur Deforge.

'Yes, yes, quite all right, just not used to heights, that's all. It'll soon pass,' returned a hesitant Wilfried, who took another careful step up the ladder as Marcel disappeared inside the vast humming vault.

The moment he passed over the threshold into the half-darkness, and before he could dwell on the ball of anguish in his belly, he felt his antennae being touched a number of times. But so far so good, he said to himself, heaving a sigh of relief. At least, nobody had bitten him yet. Then on he climbed behind Bea, toward the milling crowd on the first sallow honeycomb of three, which was suspended from the ceiling of the hollow.

Honeybees in their thousands were clambering over the golden cells, carrying out their tasks according to age and rank: from cleaning, repairing, and nursing babies, to building, sealing, ventilating with wings, and delivering provisions. Following Bea he carefully crawled vertically up the nearest flank of the honeycomb where bees were few and far between then across the hexagonal cells, some containing grubs marinating in honey, others capped with white wax where nymphs were metamorphosing.

'These are the nursery cells; only baby queens are fed solely on pure royal jelly, you know. Anyway, first we must ask permission from the queen to have some.'

'Why can't we just sneak up and take some?' said Marcel.

'Because the consequences are the same for thieving as for intruding. Look, there she is!' whispered Bea, nodding over to the other side of the honeycomb where amid the ceaseless bustle the queen, much larger than any other bee, was busy inspecting cells, surrounded by her entourage. 'There are too many workers. Someone's bound to pick you out. I'd better cross over on my own,' said Bea in a low buzz and added, 'You stay here and keep a low profile.'

'What if someone notices me?' whispered Marcel.

'Well just try and look bee-ish,' she said, and off she waddled across the honeycomb toward Her Majesty.

The winged-marcel gave a 180° glance around the hive of activity, pausing from time to time, fascinated to catch large-headed bees with huge eyes, contrary to the ambient workaholism, doing nothing in particular except supping up honey. Were Bea beside him, she would have told him these were male drones whose main function in life was to wait around until the time came to honor a queen. Then on swiveling his head back round for another scan, his sight was arrested by a single bee, this time an average worker with the particularity of having a missing front claw, lumbering in his direction. His heart sank when it became clear she was definitely heading straight toward him. Taking heed of Bea's instructions, head down, he immediately tried to look as bee-ish as was humanly possible and began to improvise some rendering work on a nearby cracked cell. Using a shard of comb, he set about scooping up residue from the cell bottom. But being of male constitution, this was certainly not the thing to do in a bees' nest.

'What do you think *you're* doing?' said the bee, coming upon him. Marcel immediately pulled back from his rendering, with his heart beating nineteen to the dozen. He looked up with a speechless shrug of the shoulders and inwardly began praying Bea would turn up pretty sharpish.

'Hey, girls, there's a funny looking drone over here trying to render!' she called out.

'And a right mess he's making of it, too!' said another worker bee, galumphing up and prodding the cell wall. And before he knew it, he found himself surrounded and the center of attention of a dozen bees poking him and scowling their observations.

'He definitely looks odd,' said a third bee.

'He does have the scent of the colony though,' said the first.

'But his body odor is suspect.'

'I say he's not a drone at all.'

'An intruder in disguise!'

'He's after our honey!'

'He's after our grubs!'

'Get him out!'

Their madding babble sent his brain spinning. Then he felt the first nip on his arm, which he instantly pulled back and, raising his hands, he said, 'Wait! All right, I'm not a drone,' he cried out.

'There, I told you,' said a satisfied maiden as her sisters stood back all agape.

'I'm not a thief either; I'm a friend,' said the boy earnestly as the bees ceased their rumpus. And regaining his composure, he added for good measure, 'And I have an audience with the queen.' This was another error, however, for there is nothing a bee finds more irritating than someone blowing their own trumpet. After a short pause, the cacophony wound up again, and the maidens pronounced their sentence.

'Kick 'im out!'

'Bite off his wings!'

'Sting 'im!' they intoned in a flourish of buzzes. Then a number of them tugged at his body, making escape by flight impossible, while others turned to show their posteriors and, by consequence, the point of their lethal darts.

Trembling with horror, Marcel instinctively held up his hands to cover his face and grit his teeth in expectance of stabbing pain. However, after a few agonizing seconds, he unwrinkled an eye to see the bees suddenly calmed and waddling back to their chores with the exception of the first one, whose mandibles were still doggedly locked onto his sleeve.

'You can let go now,' said a poised, commanding voice. 'He won't fly off yet.'

The worker bee let go, touched Marcel's trembling antennae with hers, and said, 'I am sorry. No hard feelings, eh.' And then she set about her business, fixing the crack in the cell wall that he had pretended to render.

The lad now stood facing the awesome queen bee, with her attendants waiting around her. Bea at her flank took a step forward and said, 'This is the human I told you about, Your Majesty.'

'Come, human, you must excuse them. Everyone's on edge at the moment, but no harm will come to you now,' said the queen magnanimously. Marcel bowed his thanks as low as anyone could while latching on to a honeycomb. This earned him an affable invitation to crawl along beside her widthwise across it. He was tossing it over in his mind whether he should bring up the subject of Wilfried or get the royal jelly first when the queen imperiously said, 'So the fat forager was right after all. When she said she'd been conversing with a human, we thought she'd been overindulging again.' Remaining perfectly aloof to her pampering cortege, she suddenly stopped short at a set of four or five very large cells where spare queens were being reared. Swiveling her head gravely at Marcel, she asked, 'So, you want some fresh royal jelly?'

'Yes, Your Majesty,' Marcel politely replied. The queen looked him up and down skeptically.

'Hmmm, but what food gift have you brought us in exchange?'

'Food gift, Your Majesty?' gulped the lad, swallowing down the horrible feeling that something was about to turn sour.

'Did you think we give away royal jelly for free? We were hoping for a little treat.'

As she said this, a thud shuddered through the timber of the trunk, making the honeycomb tremble very slightly. Visions of Wilfried approaching the hollow with his smoker hastened Marcel's speech as he said, 'Your Majesty, what I have to exchange is more important than food and concerns the survival of the whole colony, and we must act quickly!'

'We shall be the judge of that,' she returned dubiously. 'But say your piece.'

'A man is coming up the tree with smoke to make you drowsy and to destroy the entire colony. You'd better swarm out of here while there's still time and build your nest somewhere else!'

'Huh,' said the queen, snubbing the remark, 'the hole's too small for a man to grab our honeycombs, and if he did dare put in a mitt, it would become so swollen, he wouldn't be able to get it out again!'

'But I'm telling you, he's going to smoke you first. You'll all be trapped.'

His plea was punctuated by a dreadful cry of surprise from outside the hollow followed by an offbeat betump-betump-thunking sound. The kind of sound you would expect to hear from someone falling down a ladder.

'Was that your thief?' said the queen with majesty and a flourish of irony.

But the very next moment, the general spirit of the nest seemed to darken dramatically, and the queen suddenly stood in alarm. In an instant, the general buzz wound up to a deafening howl as honeybees began peeling away from the combs in droves and converged on the entrance. Marcel pulled himself further against the honeycomb for fear of close-flying bees knocking him off. He looked about, terrified in the whirling chaos, sensing a horrible danger in his gut where foreboding had been.

'What's going on?' he shouted.

'We're under attack, giant hornets!' returned Bea.

'Scouts have been seen sniffing round lately, and now they're back in force,' blurted the bee with the missing claw, who then switched her attention to her queen.

In the midst of her swarming subjects, the queen had been sending out alarm pheromones to various sections of the nest to call up numbers to defend in replacement of those already fallen outside. More bees in Marcel's immediate vicinity began flying from their stations to join the bustling crowd at the entrance.

'Not you,' said the queen to the maimed worker. 'You and the fat forager are to escort the human out.'

Amid scores of subjects called to the defense of the nest, Marcel, flanked by Bea and the worker, swept down to the tight cluster of individuals pouring through the entrance by their thousands. He was soon at one with the surging dark sea of buzzing bees and struggling for dear life to keep his two feet shuffling forward with the ebb and flow. At last he was out and able to breathe with more ease on reaching the outer ledge of the orifice. The bright sunlight now impacted on his retinas only to project the most horrific scene unfolding before him.

At a glance, he estimated at a mere dozen the number of giant hornets hovering supremely around the hole of the tree trunk. The powerful predators advanced steadily and lordly with intimidating poise, ever closer to the entrance despite being outnumbered something like one thousand to one. To the boy's horror, the enemy led the macabre dance, which consisted of challenging bee after bee to a duel to the death. And one by one, the maidens courageously bowled in, only to be atrociously sectioned in two by the cutting edge and sovereign force of the mandibles of the indefatigable killers. Then all hell was let loose as the hornets upped their pace into a killing binge. Plunging into the massing bees, they began mechanically biting through the hordes with terrifying efficacy. Marcel stood a dozen strides from the entrance, sickened and stunned at the massacre, while an endless stream of honeybees bustled past him to certain death.

One brave little bee managed to surprise her adversary by shooting under its abdomen and got a nip at the hornet's hind leg. But the streamlined creature with lightening reflex coiled round swiftly and simply scissored the poor bee, whose head and body independently joined the growing litter of bee parts twitching at the foot of the tree.

'Fly away, Marcel,' cried Bea on joining him at last. He was staring down blankly over the ledge where Monsieur Deforge was at present helping Wilfried hobble back to the house. A morbid stench now rose up in the air, overpowering the odor of lime tree flower and honey. Bea continued, 'Now that your human friend is no longer a threat, you can come back later for your royal jelly. It'll still be fresh in the royal cells.'

'When all is calm,' added the worker behind her.

Marcel turned his head quickly with eyes now wide open and fraught with fury. 'You mean when you're all dead!' he cried, shaking himself out of his stupid torpor. 'Look, they shouldn't be fighting one-to-one, like they were carrying out nest maintenance. In a battle like this, you've got to attack in mass. Remember how we beat the hornet in the tunnel. Take me back to the queen!' commanded Marcel forcefully. But suddenly there came a dreadful loud droning, and a massive hornet at least five times the size of a bee settled on the very landing rim of the entrance, a dozen strides away from them.

'That's right ladies, line up, one at a time,' it said with a sardonic clap of mandibles then began methodically clipping bees in half as they approached. The worker turned instinctively and dutifully headed straight for the jaws of the predator as already five or six of her sisters had done before her.

'You've *got* to tell them to fight together, Bea. Come on!' hollered Marcel above the howling din, and three seconds later the two companions were landing on either side of the worker to face the terrifying hornet together.

The instant Marcel touched down, the hornet's attention was deflected from the worker bee, and the awesome creature made a lunge for the boy with its great crushing mandibles. Had he not bounded back a step the moment his foot hit the surface of the bark, he most certainly would have been sectioned at the waist. Immediately the creature's terrible dark eyes, each the size of Marcel's head, exerted a magnetic attraction to entice the lad to a duel. Standing before the sovereign tiger of insects, Marcel now fully realized to what extent a bee attacking solo had not even a beggar's chance against such a formidable predator, incontestably designed par excellence to kill. But if the honey-makers could drop their methodical approach and just crudely mob the monsters then…

'Send out the order to mass attack!' Marcel roared at the top of his voice to Bea as he dodged another attack.

The worker bee had courageously swiped out a claw and hooked onto the hornet's left mandible, which thankfully saved Marcel from another lunge. Feeling the snag, the orange-faced exterminator instinctively yanked its massive shield-like head to counterbalance the resistance and turned it back toward the worker honeybee only to find Bea now tugging at the right mandible, so preventing the jaw from snapping shut.

'Try and hold it!' cried Marcel. Spotting a chink in the hornet's armor, he sprang up onto its thorax behind its wings, while more bees flocked and flung themselves forward in unison onto its limbs. The incensed insect dashed its mandible against the woody floor and reared up, throwing Bea aside. In the same movement, it ground its jaws together slicing the remaining claw of the worker bee clean off. Then with mechanical precision, he snipped off her head.

The beast swished its merciless cutting apparatus round to Bea. With all his might, Marcel dug his knife between the giant wasp's thoracic segments. It was like prying a knife into steel plating, though thankfully the creature was made to snap the air instead of Bea as it suddenly reared up its head from the painful stab.

'Keep sending out the order! It's working,' bawled Marcel on the back of the bucking hornet. But the next moment, the perfidious killer was kicking out its legs, discarding bees from the ends of them like oversize clogs and took to the wing in a frightening drone. Marcel figured his only chance was to keep wedged behind the thorax, which, thankfully for the boy, constituted for the hornet an infuriating spot to swat. At any rate, if Marcel slipped off now, the odds were strongly against his head and body landing in the same place.

He kept a desperate hold on the creature, who was busy with a growing number of honeybees swarming round it. Marcel spotted the plump figure of Bea among them.

'Bea, keep 'em attacking together, no solo attacks!' he hollered as heads and wings were horribly disconnected at an astounding rate, but now at least the maidens were fighting in some kind of unity. Soon, with Marcel intermittently commanding Bea to keep sending out the mass attack order, the solo forays decreased, though most of the bees still held back from the final collective onslaught. It was as though they were waiting for a cue to perform an act they had never done before, and that trigger was ironically to be initiated by the hornet itself.

In an effort to silence the yapping thing jabbing at its back, the giant hornet recoiled its thorax against the abdomen, giving Marcel the choice of either being crushed to death between the two chitinous segments or slipping into flight with a high probability of getting sliced in two. But he got an idea and swiftly took his only chance. Springing up he managed to reach over the thoracic hump and slashed his knife across the nerves at the base of a hind wing. This in turn sprung back with terrific force, sending the boy hurling blindly through the air.

Desperately he tried to spread his wings against the impetus and at last felt the cool cushion of air beneath them. He turned in time to see the hornet lamely describing wide circles, clearly no longer in control of its flight trajectory, and having lost something of its sovereign bearing. Fifty bees now swarmed around it and were closing in, despite the mandibles still ferociously chomping into the pack. The compacting ball of bees gradually became one with the predator and moved like a solid mass to the crook of a branch where it settled in a buzzing, sizzling orb.

'They're frying it!' cried Bea, hovering beside Marcel who twitched an antenna in query.

But there was no time for explanations, for a dull hypnotic droning at three o'clock alerted them of another hornet drawing bees to duel from a small cluster of them politely waiting their turn on the branch where Wilfried had placed the ladder. The winged-marcel and the fat forager turned to each other then looked straight ahead where defending maidens in their hundreds thronged at the entrance of the nest, and without conferring they winged it back to join them.

'Right, do your stuff, Bea!' shouted Marcel, barely making himself heard above the buzzing tumult, and she began communicating the pheromone to convey the impulse to the maidens to attack collectively.

A few moments later found the two companions spearheading a twenty score attack force against the giant wasp. It did not look quite as put out as it ought though, thought Marcel on approach. In fact it faced them with grim fascination and perfectly unshaken from its contemptuous stance with its huge dark eyes glistening coolly in the sun.

'Charge!' bellowed Marcel, coursing forward at the head of the mighty force. Or rather, that is what he thought, until it suddenly occurred to him that something must be amiss in the rank-and-file. The heavy thrum of bees, instead of growing with intensity as they approached the enemy, was distinctly fading. Bea must have got a similar notion, for both turned their heads in unison to find nothing but thin, empty, belittling, bee-less air.

The task force was at present forming a compact ball at nine o'clock, having been sidetracked to intercept another foe that the two companions, so engrossed in their own target, had overlooked along the way.

Of course all this happened in the space of a split second. A split second that saw Marcel go from burning boldness to cold dread as the formidable hornet hovered before them. They instantly forked off at right angles from their two-abreast formation and made a spectacular U-turn.

But the hornet was not impressed. It set its powerful wings in pursuit and very soon was snapping wildly at Marcel's feet. The lad, for the life of him, zigzagged, dived, and loop-the-looped to keep the equivalent of the length of a mandible between them. But the hornet now read the lad's flight path just as well as an air stream, and all too soon Marcel sensed a looming shadow and the force of the hornet's wings pounding the air at his side.

With a livid gasp and black terror in his liver, the lad turned his head to face the dark-tinged orange jaws of death. It only had to make a dip to sever him at the neck, and the only thing the horror-struck Marcel could do was tuck his head into his shoulders. The merciless predator indeed swished its head, snapped its mandibles together, and despite the boy's sharp swerve away from the lunge, clipped a piece out of his wing, knocking him off balance a moment. The creature was preparing to deliver the *coup de grace* when out of the blue the hornet stopped dead in mid-flight, leaving Marcel alone, zooming through the suddenly darkened air, thick with honeybees spearheaded by Bea.

The whirling orb of bees opened up and closed behind the winged-marcel as he passed through. Once at the tail end, despite the nick in his wing, he outlined another nifty U-turn zooming round to see the maidens surround the surprised hornet. However, the creature quickly recovered its composure and defiantly hovered at the core of the bee-ish ball, and with every deliberate lunge, clipped off a head like someone pruning a rose-bush. Marcel then perceived Bea now at the front line, dodging lunges with her sisters, clearly hesitant as to how to go about apprehending the foe.

'Grab it from behind first,' roared the boy, blazing his way through the crowd and hurled himself into the hornet's thorax from behind. Suddenly something clicked into place, and before he knew it, bees were piling on with him, while others arrested limbs, wings, and mandibles. They then conveyed the captive to the nearest fork in the tree, where they proceeded in vibrating their wing muscles. This had the extraordinary effect of raising the temperature of the orb of bees to a stifling degree.

So this is what Bea meant about frying it, thought Marcel as he struggled to free himself from the roasting melee that engulfed the hornet.

The mass attack pheromone spread like wildfire, and all about bees were rallying into whirling battalions and overcoming a fourth, a fifth, a sixth, and then a seventh giant hornet, these last two being cunningly lured into the nest where they were more easily dealt with. But the remaining four hornets escaped with their lives.

22
A Royal Recompense

From a honeybee's point of view, if the most refreshing dip of the day is undisputedly to be had early morning, the most exquisite will be got in the late afternoon. Then the sun has lost its sting enough to make harvesting a joy and has mollified the flowers to a tee, making their nectar even more sweet and fluid. The hum in the air was at its height with hosts of forager bees avidly dipping into the lime tree flower cups. A faint stream of summer breeze, accompanied by the sound of a motor car and girls' laughter, made the foliage quiver in places along the driveway that ran between the lime trees up to the west side of Villeneuve.

But at the nest in the great lime tree on the east side, that finest moment had been given over to savoring an even sweeter taste—the taste of victory. And a thousand times Marcel was stopped and hailed a hero.

'Thank you, but have you seen my friend, Bea, you know, the fat forager?' he invariably asked, putting a brave face on his dark worries.

Meanwhile, before the house, the Panhard delivered its carriage safely to port, but before the handbrake was pulled to its full position, a carriage door was swung open and the cheerful banter was immediately extinguished by a short sharp scream.

'No! They've taken the bees already!' cried a very distraught young woman now running across the lawn toward the ladder propped against the lime tree.

The barrel-hipped lady holding the wheel stood up in surprise while round the corner the side door to the kitchen opened and Monsieur Deforge's head stuck out.

'Henriette, STOP! There are hornets,' he roared. 'Come and help. Young Wilfried's fallen and done something to his ankle.' This was enough to stop her in her tracks. Indeed, at that moment in time, there was not another soul alive more pleased to hear of someone suffering from a wounded ankle than Henriette.

'Don't just stand there gawking, girl, come and help,' bellowed her father. Her relief turned to concern as she hurried across the lawn with her cousin now supporting her at her waist.

'Blasted bees. I've sent for someone to finish the job,' said the booming voice of Deforge as his daughter and niece swept through the kitchen door, while up in the lime tree, Marcel disappeared back inside the buzzing nest.

The smell of lime honey was stronger than ever, and honeybees were flocking in their droves to the upper part of the honeycombs where their wings wafted down the delicious odor. On the brood side, the lower part where eggs were laid and siblings were reared, Bea stood proudly with the queen in the middle of a cluster of admiring attendants and workers, thoroughly enjoying her moment of glory. Marcel had just joined them amid congratulations, and glad he was, too, to find his companion alive and buzzing.

'But what pheromone did you use?' the queen asked.

'Actually, it isn't one we are taught, Your Majesty. I call it a mass attack pheromone,' said Bea loftily and thoroughly reveling in her own cleverness.

The queen marked a pause, and with a note of suspicion, she asked, 'If you didn't know it already, then how did you come about it?' The change of tone was hardly perceptible but was enough to put a damper on the jubilant hum. If foragers were capable of making up pheromones, wasn't her leadership at stake, and, consequently, the whole spirit of the bee colony with it?

'Well, actually,' said Bea, coming down from her high perch, 'the winged-marcel told me we must fight together.' Then she turned to Marcel as if to prompt his backing.

'But we have a pheromone for that,' said the queen before Marcel could stir.

'This pheromone not only prompts us to fight together but also all at once, Your Majesty,' said Bea. 'It's the only way to overcome giant hornets.'

'That's all well and good, but normally it's my job to think up pheromones.'

'If you don't mind my saying, Your Majesty,' said Marcel, sensing the queen's susceptibility, 'it's quite normal that you didn't. I mean, given that you haven't dealt with giant hornets before. In fact these hornets are from a faraway land; they shouldn't be here at all. You see, it's the fault of humans that they are here, so it is only right that a human should provide you with a defense strategy. And the only defense against them is to mob them. Besides,' continued Marcel in a sudden inspiration, 'take it as my humble gift to Your Majesty and the colony.'

'Hmmm, a gift,' returned the queen, twirling her antennae as if turning over the notion in her brain. Now that she was quite satisfied that the idea had not germinated in the forager's mind after all, she said in a decidedly cheerier tone, 'Yes, a gift, we accept gifts, and indeed it is a gift worthy of a royal recompense, young human. And you shall have what you came for!' This immediately raised everyone's spirits again. She turned to her attendants to give the command to them in a secret language conveyed by her glands and feelers. Meanwhile Marcel's attention was diverted to the upper part of the honeycomb where bees were now breaking open wax seals and gorging themselves with honey stored in the hexagonal compartments. After a moment the queen spoke again.

'There are two, in case you lose one. Fresh royal jelly is trapped inside so that you can carry it with you outside the tree,' she said after handing him two wax balls. 'And make sure you do, otherwise, if what the forager says is true, you will never fit through the entrance, and we shall be pushed for space!' said the queen warmly, which caused an affable buzz.

But it was with gravity that Marcel took the wax balls and said, 'Thank you, Your Majesty. We may have saved the colony, but you know you really must leave the nest quickly. Some of the hornets got away; they will be back in greater numbers. And besides that, the man of the house will not let you stay here; I heard him say so.'

The queen glanced up at the bees clustering around the honey cells and switched back to Marcel. 'That is precisely what we are doing. That is why we are filling ourselves with provisions. But even so, we cannot leave until the scouts have found a suitable settlement, and all that takes time.'

'But time is short, the hornets will be back sooner than later. I can feel it in my chitin, Your Majesty.'

'Without provisions the colony will die; we will never find enough resources to feed a new generation.'

'Your Majesty,' intervened Bea hesitantly, 'I meant to say so sooner, but with all the commotion and everything…it must have slipped my mind.'

'Spit it out then!' urged the queen.

'I came across a whole field of sunflowers nearby, which have already started to open,' said Bea meekly. 'It's a place where we won't need to take so many provisions, because there are thousands and thousands of them.'

On the mention of the highly prized flower, Marcel recalled Bea's sunflowered appearance on her return from her 'test flight.' She had evidently been to Mon Plaisir field at the rear of the house.

'Sunflowers, already!' exclaimed the queen, both euphoric and fretful as anyone would be on finding out they were camping right near a field with pots of gold up for grabs.

'Yes, Your Majesty.'

'You have done well, forager. We must send out scouts there immediately to mark the best place for our nest, before any other colony gets wind!'

'I know the field well, Your Majesty,' said Marcel. 'You can build your nest in the old elm on the nearest corner of the field from here. I know for sure that the farmer will be glad to have you. His harvest will be all the better for your company.'

Bea regurgitated and exchanged nectar as proof of her claim, did a short waggle dance, which was faithfully performed across the nest by the workers who saw it, and very soon every bee in the colony was buzzing with the imminent prospect of departure to a promised land flowing with sunflower nectar.

***

A short time later, Marcel looked admiringly at the incredible spectacle of legions of honeybees swarming into the air and wondered how they managed to fly so close together.

'Good luck and fair wind,' he yelled from the threshold of the nest in response to a last glance back from Bea. This he instantly regretted as the recollection of her midair collision with Rhino struck him. But this time, thankfully, everyone was travelling the same way and, taking pride of place beside her queen, she soon disappeared amid the thickening cluster of honeybees.

He watched them fly between the boughs of the lime tree and pass the house, which was already blocking out a good slice of the westering sun. And on they wended over the roof of the stables without stopping toward the great elm on Mon Plaisir field where the flowers still had a couple of hours of sunning before they would start turning in their petals for the night.

***

The late afternoon sun filled the air with a blithe warmth, lending every particle it touched a copperish hue and diffusing that soulful comfort so particular to southern continental skies. Marcel had shifted further along the branch, where he was able to get a full view of the grand old oak at the far end of the grounds in all its glory.

Dangling his legs three meters up over the edge of his perch, he now scanned the gilt-tinged meadow in an attempt to retrace his path. He rolled his eyes up to the front of the house, where old Malzac was taking care of the motor car, skimmed them over the lily pond full of languid effervescence, and followed a fluttering butterfly with them to the flower garden, all in the space of a slow turn of the head.

Yet what an incredible voyage it had been, and to think that it was only yesterday he had started out from the great oak tree. He had come so far in many ways. No longer did he doubt his resourcefulness, not as long as he kept up the will to prevail. He truly felt now, smugly perhaps, that his future lay in his own hands. And to get the ball rolling, he only had to crack the wax-sealed royal jelly onto his tongue, and his metamorphosis into a young man, without means but with dreams, would begin. Yep, his whole future was locked up in the ball he now held up to the sun. The other sat snugly in his pocket.

Marcel sat there a few moments more, wondering where exactly he should do it, metamorphose, that is. At all costs, he figured, he must do it at ground level. Even for a full-size lad, three meters is one long way to fall.

He popped the wax ball into his inner blazer pocket with its twin. Then he spread his wings to hug the soft warm air for the last time. *Maybe I ought to get back to the oak tree*, he mused, gliding freely on an upward air current. With wings, he would be there in no time. *Hah, or maybe I could go for a last tour of the grounds, get full use out of my wings before they're gone forever.* After all,

technically speaking, he still had another two moons.
'Hmm, what if I paid a visit to Julia,' he said to himself with a crafty chuckle while saluting winged insects zooming the other way.

But all of a sudden, a deep drone, getting louder and louder, hummed through the air, smiting out his syrupy thoughts and sending a chill of horror through his blood. Frantically, he scoured the vicinity to make out its position, when clean out of the sun, the orange-tinged silhouette of a giant hornet came coursing straight at him. Giving full thrust to his wings, Marcel dipped into a vertical nosedive and looped back to a cluster of lime tree flowers to keep a solid distance between them. *Why didn't I just land there and eat the bloody ball?* He could have kicked himself for being so stupid. He had been too complacent, that's what.

After winging it round the cluster again, the massive hornet just bowled through the flimsy vegetal barrier while Marcel smartly doubled back and zigzagged between leafy twigs, scathing a wing on one of them while fumbling desperately in his inner pocket. Again the boy dodged the abominable predator and, for the last time, he sensed the formidable killer looming over him as he quickly crushed a wax ball between his teeth. The smoothest, sweetest impression flowed over his tongue, but in the fury of the chase, he was in no mind to enjoy it. There immediately followed another sensation that prevailed over all others as he felt a terrible jab pierce his back. An intense burning pain instantly devoured his entire being, while a whirling kaleidoscope of light and color sped past his eyes. Then all light was snuffed out for the winged-marcel.

23

Spreading Wings

It was a full-grown Marcel Dassaud who opened his eyes at last to find himself in bed in a dark room. The familiar fragrance allowed him to suspect he was on the east side of Villeneuve, having slept there many a time as a young boy. In the summer the spare room was used for drying heaps of lime flowers for the concoction of autumnal nightcaps. Drowsily he propped himself up on his elbows a few moments before proceeding unsteadily across the room, guided by a slit of bright light.

The moment he pushed open the wooden shutters, the summer's day flooded in, causing him to squint and hold up a hand as a shield. His next impulse was to examine his palms, which were smooth, paw his head, which presented only one lump at the back, and pinch his chest, which was soft and pale. He was trying to catch his back in the long mirror of the mahogany wardrobe when a bee came bumbling in, nosed around the room, and bumbled back out. All of a sudden, there came a rumbling that rolled up the staircase, and in the next minute, the door sprung open and in poured Julia and Henriette with Wilfried hobbling in after them.

'We heard the shutters, how you feeling?' said Julia in her usual spirited manner.

'Er? Oh, all right,' replied Marcel groggy-headed. 'Pity my wings have gone, though,' he added, touching his back. The two girls gave a dubious glance at one another, while Marcel winced on discovering a bump on his back.

'He's probably still delirious,' was Julia's diagnosis. 'Come on,' she beckoned. Seconded by Henriette, she helped him back to his bed. She told him he had been found in a heap on the ground, having been stung by one of those giant hornets that were infesting the region.

'We found your hat under the oak tree first and wondered where you'd disappeared to,' added Henriette.

Marcel still had a vague look about him, but the mention of the oak tree seemed to open a door in his memory, and he now pictured himself strolling along to his favorite pondering place where, he surmised, he must have fallen asleep. Absently he dabbed his fingers over the tender lump through the gauze on his lower back as a mix of weird scenes flickered through his mind.

'That's where you got stung, Marcel,' said Julia matronly.

'The doctor gave you quite hefty doses of sedative to get you over the worst of it,' said Henriette.

'You got up to a roaring temperature,' said Julia, taking a seat on the edge of his bed.

'I've heard four of those hornets can kill a horse, you know,' said Wilfried, standing behind Henriette and added, 'so you've been lumped here, mate. Julia's been fretting about you most. She's been in and out the whole time.'

'And she's the one who got your pajamas for you,' said Henriette.

'Don't worry, though, it was the nurse who came and did you up.'

'All right, Wilfried, you needn't go into the details,' said Julia with a playful frown.

But the excited chatter seemed to float around Marcel's ears in a mingled babbling as he became more and more drawn into fleeting visions of a strange dream. And, quite the opposite to what dreams usually do, those snippets became longer and clearer as they came back to him, more like a memory. The recollection of his antennae was so vivid now that he could virtually feel them on his head as he scratched it groggily, although it still thankfully presented no outgrowths.

At least one thing was certainly real though, and that was the newfound meaning to his life that the dream had left him. He definitely felt galvanized by his fantastic 'metamorphosis' and could distinctly feel a new mettle inside as sure as he was sitting on the bed in the spare bedroom at Villeneuve now.

He glanced at Henriette, sitting on one side of him, and noticed a new dimension to her; maybe it was her hair being released from her plait and flowing over her shoulders. At any rate, she seemed more colorful than before, less withdrawn, and she was actually giggling and enjoying herself. It was as though she had metamorphosed over night, too. He noticed that from time to time she reached furtively behind her back to catch Wilfried's hand as though to reassure herself he was still there. So their mutual affection was not just a figment of his dream. It certainly seemed to support the reality of his insect adventure.

Slipping in and out of his fantastic reverie, he was beginning to lose the frontier between the real and the imagined as his gaze settled again on Julia, speaking away beside him. But her warmth and magnetism, making him want to reach out and touch her hand, gradually pulled him back into the present.

At last, in a pause in the excited babble, Marcel spoke.

'Well,' he said slowly, 'you'll never believe it, but I dreamt I turned into an insect. I had wings, and I could fly.'

In a few words, he zealously recounted the start of his adventures across the meadow. His listeners intermittently gave each other dubious looks, which probably translated their concern for his mental health. Then Wilfried tactfully interrupted his narrative with a quip.

'The doctor did say there might be some immediate side effects to the sedative, but I s'pose it was better than putting you out with a sledge hammer!'

'You were awfully feverish, Marcel,' added Henriette. 'We were all worried for you, weren't we, Julia?'

'Now that's enough nonsense, Marcel Dassaud, and listen to me,' said Julia, taking control of the situation. Then, in an effort to win him back to reason, she placed her hands on his shoulders, which to Marcel was bewitching enough, and teasingly said, 'You haven't been turned into a bug yet; you've just been stung by one, silly. Right?' Before Marcel could put up any resistance, heavy footsteps on the landing announced Monsieur Deforge's arrival before he swung open the door.

'Hah, Marcel, dear boy, you gave us all quite a fright,' he said and recounted how the beekeeper, alerted by none other than Chico, had come upon him lying amid the undergrowth on the thicket side of the lime tree.

'You mean I wasn't under the oak tree?' questioned Marcel, who up until then had fallen to believing that he had been found under the great oak, which would have made sense if he had somehow fallen asleep there before getting stung.

'No, the lime tree, my boy, probably fell out of it. Whatever were you doing? Picking lime flowers, were you? Or trying to get a look at the bees?' Marcel counted yet another uncanny coincidence in the nonsense of his dream while returning a blank nod at Monsieur Deforge.

'Nasty things, hornets, you know. Young Wilfried fell clean down the ladder as soon as he set his eyes on one, didn't you, Wilfried?'

'Yes, sir, and a good job I did, too,' said the scout with a glance to Henriette.

'I was worried you wouldn't make it to the party, my boy,' said Deforge, turning back to Marcel.

The party—Marcel knew what that meant. He looked straight at his interlocutor and this time with calm conviction he said, 'I'm sorry, Monsieur Deforge, but I can't stay on here at Villeneuve after all.'

'What are you talking about, Marcel?'

'My future is elsewhere…in Paris…I've won a scholarship.'

'B, bu, but,' clucked Deforge, 'we had an agreement. We'll speak about it once you've rested.'

'My mind is made up, and besides that, it wouldn't be right to take the limelight at Henriette's birthday party, would it? And I, er, think she has something to say,' Marcel concluded, giving the cue to Henriette, sensing somehow the time was ripe for her to confront her father.

'Father, if Marcel wants to better himself, then he must. Haven't you always said how clever he is? Besides, he'll come back and see us during the holidays.'

'Yes, b, but—'

'And there's another thing, I do have my own announcement to make at my party, and I think you ought to know first. Father, I'm no longer a child,' she said hesitantly but with determination all the same.

'What are you going on about, girl?'

'I'm a woman, Father, and Wilfried and I have plans—together.'

'Wilfried?'

'Yes, sir, with all due respect, I love your daughter,' said Wilfried, standing upright and bravely placing an arm around Henriette's waist. 'My parents will be glad to have her in our family.'

Deforge looked blankly from the lanky scout to his daughter and then to Marcel, quite flabbergasted as to the workings of human metamorphosis and quite surprised to suddenly see before him, not the bunch of kids he once thought he knew, but budding teenagers on the verge of spreading their wings. Suddenly the puff was taken out of him and, holding his chin, he nodded his head as if to concede defeat.

At length he cast a more clement glance toward Marcel and said, 'Your father would have wanted you to go on learning; he would have been proud. Remember, fortune favors the brave, my boy. Just do your best, and you will be fine.' Then, taking a step over to Henriette, he said, 'Well, you'd better get a move on. It won't be long before your guests start to arrive, my little lady.' And he lowered his powerful head and kissed his daughter on the forehead. At last the nymph had hatched, and the truth was he had been half hoping she would one day assert herself, otherwise, how would his only offspring pass on the Deforge grit? It was a grave but, nevertheless, appeased Philibert Deforge who left the four friends to their growing up.

As the door was pulled to, Marcel, half cottoning on to Deforge's last words, said, 'What are your guests arriving already for?'

'For the party tonight, silly,' said Julia, who had moved over to embrace Henriette.

'Euh? What day is it then?' he said, suddenly panicked in the knowledge that he had to send off his acceptance before noon Saturday.

'What day?' said Julia. 'Oh, yes, I nearly forgot, you've been in and out of consciousness at least since the beekeeper found you.'

'Which was precisely thirty-seven hours and fifteen minutes ago,' added Wilfried, looking at his timepiece.

'Which makes it Saturday, by the way, all day long. And fifteen minutes to eleven to be precise.'

'What? You're joking? I haven't sent my letter of acceptance!'

'Really?' asked Julia, not showing the least bit of concern.

'I haven't even written it, and now it's too flippin' late, I'll never make it to the post office in time. What am I going to do?' said the lad, holding his head.

'Yes, too late now, which is why I sent it yesterday, Marcel Dassaud!'

A wave of relief washed over Marcel's face as he looked up at Julia. 'I don't know what I'm going to do in Paris without you,' he said, which flushed his cheeks the moment the words came out. It was the bare truth, though; he didn't know how he would manage without seeing her.

Julia and Henriette gave a knowing giggle. 'Actually, I was hoping you'd come and see me play sometimes,' said Julia playfully. Marcel let out an incomprehensible sound, which echoed his puzzlement.

'She's taking up her lessons at the Paris Conservatoire,' said Henriette.

'How come? I thought—'

'We were too poor to afford it? Well, so did I until yesterday. One of Daddy's patents has been taken up by an industrialist,' she said with a contained laugh in her voice.

'That's brilliant; so you'll be in Paris, too,' said Marcel with a broad grin. Then he added more soberly, 'Well, I mean, I s'pose it shows that sticking to your convictions somehow pays in the end, right?'

Julia had grabbed Marcel's blazer from a wooden chair and now holding it up. 'And the first thing you'll be needing is a new jacket, Marcel. Looks like you've outgrown this one,' she said revealing a great gaping rip down the middle in the back of it. Everyone laughed out loud as, of all things, a tiny winged-insect caught Marcel's eye, and with a secret grin, he watched it fly across the room and out through the window. It was a Cynips, otherwise known as a gallfly.